Praise for Stephen Elli

"*Happy Baby* is surely the n   ...gent and beautiful book ever written about juvenile detention centers, sadomasochism, and drugs." —Curtis Sittenfeld, *New York Times*

"Stephen Elliott's *Happy Baby* brings a rare degree of intelligence and literary accomplishment to the story of Theo, a veteran of brutal Chicago group homes, hopelessly mangled relationships and random violence. Though told in the lean, emotionally terse language of the contemporary trauma memoir, there's not a speck of self-pity here, just a wincing, dogged search for the truth. What's brave about Theo isn't his willingness to examine and detail his own sufferings; it's his determination to understand how they have shaped him and his refusal to allow them to define him." —Salon.com, Ten Best Books of the Year 2004

10·21·8

"*Happy Baby* offers us the lives of 'the ugliest and the weakest,' of those always sitting at the back of the room, in the corners, the gutters, the bombed-out and burned-down palaces of the soul. Reading it we descend into a psycho-sexual-social nightmare and, because of Elliott's masterful and vivid storytelling, we land in grace." —Anthony Swofford, author of *Jarhead*

"By telling [*Happy Baby*] backward, Elliott puts us in a position of wanting to know/dreading the knowledge, and it's a graceful strategy that gives *Happy Baby* its unique veracity and humane edge." —*Village Voice*

"Good fiction satisfies; great fiction challenges. Stephen Elliott's third novel, *What It Means to Love You,* is without question a rough, often painful journey through the steamy underworld of Chicago, yet the trip is infinitely rewarding." —*Austin American Statesman*

"Elliot's [*Happy Baby*] recalls a life defined by longing for both love and pain. Blending the edginess of Augusten Burroughs with the raw emotion of Marguerite Duras, this compelling confessional reveals a ravaged soul seeking solace and resolution in the wake of unspeakable crimes." —Allison Block, *Booklist*

"[Stephen Elliot's] ability to capture the fragile sensibility of troubled youth is uncanny...and his descriptions of life on the streets are crookedly lyrical." —*Publishers Weekly*

My Girlfriend
Comes to the City
and Beats Me Up

My Girlfriend
Comes to the City
and Beats Me Up

by

STEPHEN ELLIOTT

CLEIS
PRESS

Published in the United States by Cleis Press Inc., P.O. Box 14697, San Francisco, California 94114.

Printed in the United States.
Cover design: Scott Idleman
Cover illustration: Laurenn McCubbin
Book design: Karen Quigg
Cleis Press logo art: Juana Alicia
First Edition.
10 9 8 7 6 5 4 3 2 1

"First Things First," "What It's Like in San Francisco" (under the title "San Francisco Love Story"), and "My Girlfriend Comes to the City and Beats Me Up" originally appeared in Nerve.com. "What It's Like in San Francisco" also appeared in *Best American Erotica 2006.* "My Stripper Year" originally appeared in the anthology *Sex Worker Art Show.* "Other Desires" originally appeared in *McSweeney's* 11 and as a chapter in *Happy Baby.* "Tears" originally appeared in *Scarlet Letters.* "Three Men and a Woman" originally appeared in the *New York Times.* "My Friend Petey" originally appeared in *Story Quarterly.* "Just Always Be Good" originally appeared in *Tin House* and *Best Sex Writing 2006.*

Library of Congress Cataloging-in-Publication Data

Elliot, Shephen, 1971–
    My girlfriend comes to the city and beats me up / by Stephen Elliot. — 1st ed.
       p. cm.
    ISBN-13: 978-1-57344-255-8 (pbk. : alk. paper)
    ISBN-10: 1-57344-255-0 (pbk. : alk. paper)
1. Man-woman relationships—Fiction. 2. San Francisco (Calif.)—Fiction. I. Title.
    PS3605.L46M9   2006
    813'.6—dc22   2006016839

ACKNOWLEDGMENTS

I'd like to thank Susan Harrison, Michelle Orange, and Rita Rich for the early reads of this manuscript; Frédérique Delacoste and Felice Newman at Cleis Press for providing a home for this book; and Laurenn McCubbin —my favorite artist—for the cover illustration. There are many more people I would like to thank but who prefer not to have their name on a dirty book; here's hoping they change their mind before the next one.

Love never dies a natural death. It dies because we don't know how to replenish its source. It dies of blindness and errors and betrayals. It dies of illness and wounds. It dies of weariness, of withering, of tarnishing. —Anaïs Nin

What belongs to Greatness. Who can attain to anything great if he does not feel in himself the force and will to inflict great pain? The ability to suffer is a small matter... But not to perish from internal distress and doubt when one inflicts great suffering and hears the cry of it—that is great, that belongs to greatness. —Friedrich Nietzsche

Contents

Introduction:
This Could Have Been a Memoir

THIS COULD HAVE BEEN A MEMOIR. It isn't. Most of it is true. This could have been a *sexual memoir*. Ultimately, I made the poor marketing choice of calling this a book of stories because there were too many things in it I knowingly made up. With the exception of "Three Men and a Woman," "My Stripper Year," and "Just Always Be Good," which were originally published as nonfiction, nearly every story in this collection has already been published as fiction. Real life does not always finish as neatly as fiction. Also, as I say in "I'll Love You Back," I didn't want to be responsible for the truth of my recollections.

But the reason I am admitting here, in this introduction, to the general if not complete truth of this book, is because I believe in being open about sexuality.

Recently there has been a rash of crackdowns on prac-
titioners of consensual sadomasochism. Our president,
who sanctions torture all over the world, who threatens
to veto bills banning the American military from torture,
has initiated a war at home on people who like to tie and
hurt each other in the privacy of their own bedrooms.
In response to the Department of Justice crackdown on
S/M websites many sex educators have taken down their
pages. The result is that people who are just beginning
their explorations in the world of bondage and discipline are going to find good information advocating safe
and consensual play harder to find. When that happens
beginners are more likely to play without safe words;
to engage in dangerous activities, like cutting and
asphyxiation, with partners who are not properly
trained. And people are going to continue to live
unhappy and ashamed of their desires when they could
be leading satisfying and passionate lives.

It is in everyone's best interest for more people to
be open about their sexual desires. More pride flags
need to be displayed on porches and windows and tattoos. As kinky people we need to talk to our nonkinky
friends about our desires. We can't wait for the approval
of others; we must force them to accept us. We will never
have political power until we let the politicians know
that we are not ashamed.

With that in mind I take responsibility for these
stories, for every sexual act depicted, many of which

occurred when I was younger, before I made the effort to acquire the information I needed. I acquired scars instead. This is not a memoir, but it's damn close. And I'm OK with that. And I'm OK with you knowing that.

Stephen Elliott
May 2006

First Things First

THE GRASSHOPPER YOUTH HOSTEL in Amsterdam was three stories high and appeared like an old red brick mansion rising over the third canal. Green lights climbed the walls like vines and gargoyles perched on the corners, their talons digging into the cement. It cost eight dollars a night to bunk in dorm rooms with twenty beds and was located on the Warmoesstraat, near the Old Church and the Terminus where the streets were slick with vomit, beer, and urine.

Outside everything was for sale and pickpockets followed you watching to see where you held your wallet. There was always a party at night, neon marijuana leaves in the windows, gays in chaps and shirtless women cruising out front. Junkies sat on bags of garbage sticking their arms. Near the bridges students played guitar while their friends waved hats and asked for change. There were jugglers and sex shows and the authorities had not yet cracked down on the illegal immigrants sitting in lingerie in rented doorways along the Oudezijds.

The clerk at the Grasshopper was a large Moroccan with a helmet of curly black hair. He was arguing with two men in the entrance. They wanted to see one of the hostel tenants.

"He's not here," the clerk said. He sounded impatient. If he turned to reach the phone one of them would slip past to the upper floors.

"That's impossible he isn't here," the smaller one told the clerk as if speaking to a child. "Because he owes us money."

One of the men arguing at the counter turned and stared at me, sizing me up, weighing my value while his friend pleaded their case. His friend hammered his fist on the counter. "Get out," the man behind the counter said.

"Look at him," the smaller one said to me, baring his teeth, spittle gathering in the corner of his mouth. "He doesn't understand. Why not?"

A woman stood near the yellow lockers with a magazine in her hand and a bored expression on her face. She was old compared to me, and not pretty. I was only twenty, and traveling on a one-way ticket. She had thick shoulders, a football player's body, and short spiky hair that had gone grey in patches. If her face wasn't so weathered and pockmarked and sturdy it might have resembled a young boy's. She wore black boots and a leather skirt without stockings. Her skin was the color of clay.

I paused for a moment on the bottom stair, then approached the woman and told her I had seen her earlier at the bar on the end of the canal. There were rules at that bar for what people could and could not wear so I had not worn a shirt. I sat half naked in the corner in a deep black chair and drank a Coke. She had been on a platform at the far end torturing a red-haired man. His arms were chained above his head and he was blindfolded. He had a pointy beard; his body was soft and shapeless, impossible to see where his chest ended and his stomach began. She had covered him in clothespins, which she twisted and squeezed.

"I don't remember you," she said. I smiled and looked at the floor, trying to hide my panic. "I think I would remember you. What were you doing in *that* bar?" she asked.

The man near the counter turned his attention back to the clerk.

Outside was cold. I walked with her to her hotel. I don't think she gave me her name but if she did I forgot it right away. "You should have a scarf in this weather," she told me.

We walked across the bridges and down the Voorburg to where the lights ended. I was glad to be away from the men at the counter. I felt safe with this woman because she was Dutch and her body was so sturdy. I didn't ask her what she was doing in the youth hostel. She told me she wasn't from Amsterdam; she lived somewhere near Rotterdam. She had come to Amsterdam for a party, and she asked if I knew about the party that was going to happen in a couple of days. "A big event," she said.

I told her I didn't know about it.

The Royal Kabul was on the edge of the red-light district, just past the Moulin Rouge and the sex museum, near the Zeedijk. The streets around the hotel were very quiet and all of the windows facing the street were dark. I stopped at the entrance, my hands tucked in my pockets. I was scared that she would tell me I couldn't come in with her and I would have to walk back. There was no safe way back to the hostel at night. Along the canal was a low green rail and people were pushed over sometimes and beaten when they climbed out wet on the other side. She knew what she wanted to do but she let a few moments pass. "You can come into the bar and I'll buy you a drink. But you'll have to dance for me." Which is what I did. I danced for her.

I danced with my eyes closed a couple of feet away from her while she sat on a stool with a glass of rum. There was a beer next to her but when I tried to pick it up she said, "No, dance first." I worried a little that if I danced too far away one of the hotel managers would collar me, and demand to see my room key, which of course I didn't have. I thought if I was behind other people, and she couldn't see me, then she wouldn't notice them walking me out with their hands on my elbows and the back of my neck and I knew she wouldn't come looking for me. She would see I was gone and presume I had just run off, changed my mind. Nobody ever looks for you when you disappear except on television. In real life they let you go and then forget. She would shrug her shoulders and go back to her room and I would be left to my own devices. So I stayed close, as close as I could, and when I got close enough she reached out and grabbed me by my belt and pulled me forward so I was dancing over her leg and she put her hand on my ass and whispered, "I think you and I might have some things in common." Then she pinched my earlobe and I let out a quick yelp.

In her room she was very formal. There was a dresser and a black case and a window with the curtain pulled. She didn't ask what I liked, which was good because I had no idea what I liked or what I was into or what I wanted to do or wanted done to me. "Take your clothes off and put them in the corner. Come on." She snapped her fingers beneath my nose. She seemed to think I had been through this before, but I hadn't. I had been arrested as a child and I spent three months in a mental hospital when I was fourteen, but that was all. "Raise your arms, spread your legs, turn around." She ran her hands over my arms and between my legs, searching me until she was satisfied. She tied me to the bed faceup with rope and rubber straps and pulled a hood over my head so I couldn't see anything. There was a hole for my mouth. She tied my cock and balls together and told me to stick my tongue out and then slapped my face hard, the way my father used to. "Stick your tongue out further," she said. "Good. Stay like that."

I knew it was a knife right away, as soon as I felt the cold on my leg. She had run a rope over my neck so I couldn't lift my head. I felt the knife working its way across my body, not quite cutting me. I knew the knife was sharp, I felt my skin wanting to break. Then I felt the first cut. "Just a little blood," she said. "For me." She drew the knife below my penis and lifted my balls with the flat side of the blade. All of my muscles tensed and I started to cry inside the hood.

"Relax," she said. "There's nothing you can do one way or the other. Breathe." She waited but I couldn't catch my breath. She pulled the knife away, then gripped my balls tightly in her fist and I screamed.

"I said breathe. Breathe for your mommy." I tried to focus. I tried to breathe, and I finally did, I breathed in large, deep breaths, and she loosened her grip. I thought of the couch in the living room where I grew up and my mother lying there under a knit blanket for many years. "That's better. That's what mommy wants. You only have a couple of cuts on your leg and you're crying already.

Now I'm going to put something in your mouth so you don't scream again."

I didn't know anything about safe words then. She peeled the hood to just below my nose. The gag was a large plastic puck with a hole in the center of it and it stretched my cheeks painfully and hurt more still when she pulled the hood back over my face. I heard the snap of the lighter and smelled the smoke. First her finger poked through the mouth hole in the mask and the puck and she ran her fingernail over my tongue, pressed it down. Then she flicked the ashes in my mouth. I could hear the paper burn away at the edges every time she took a drag and I was only able to moan like some doomed animal when she lowered the finished cigarette onto my ribs, dotting it out across my skin.

At some point, it may have been hours, she untied me and plucked the gag from my cheeks. I was very weak and tired and my body was shaking involuntarily and she turned me over. "Onto your knees," she said. "Like a puppy dog. That's a good boy." She placed pillows beneath my stomach and smeared me in Vaseline and she entered me from behind with her strap-on. She did it slowly, very slowly, and it didn't hurt as much as it might have. I had never been entered before. She leaned across my back, wrapping one arm around my chest and gripping my neck with her other hand, occasionally squeezing my windpipe so I couldn't breathe for a second. I cried again, but it was a different crying. I was very comfortable. I don't think I had ever been comfortable before. She rubbed her hand over my face, washing my cheeks with my tears. "Yes," she said. "Cry some more. I like that very much." When she was done I slept curled in a ball facing her, my forehead against her collarbone, her heavy arm across my shoulder.

Early in the morning, while the city was still dark, I got dressed and shouldered my pack. I pushed the curtain and saw a deep red over the tops of the buildings like the edge of a bruise. I couldn't go back to America. I didn't know where I could go. I opened the leather case and saw all of the sharp tools, gags, dildos, wrist cuffs, chains, iodine, needles, latex gloves, and several hundred dollars. She was sleeping and I considered taking her money. I had already robbed a man who had taken me home in London. We'd met at an upscale bar in Chelsea, there was a strip contest and the winner received the loudest applause from the crowd. "Cheer for me," I told him, before stepping onto the podium, but all he did was clap politely as I stripped to my underwear, so I lost. He said he was a chef for the French Embassy and I went home with him but I asked him not to touch me. I said there would be time for that later but I was just stalling. I took a wool sweater from him and a small pile of twenty-pound notes.

She was still wearing her boots and leather skirt and sleeping peacefully. I watched her sleeping for a while. I didn't know anything about her except that she was heavy, too heavy to lift, and she lived somewhere else. I closed the case and bit my lip. I didn't understand what I was feeling. I thought it was an urge to be buried alive or drowned but it was probably a desire to crawl back into bed and stay.

I left and I walked straight to the Terminus and boarded a train to Berlin. In Berlin I rented a very small room just east of the wall, which had been torn down recently. People were painting all over the sides of buildings, giant murals everywhere. I sat in that room in East Berlin for two weeks listening to German radio and sleeping and masturbating until my penis was lined with friction sores and broken skin. When I finally made it back to Amsterdam I couldn't find her. Holland is a small country but I wasn't from there. I went to the Royal Kabul but I didn't even have her name. She didn't live there. She was gone.

My Stripper Year

FIRST THERE WAS TONI in his sparkling cocktail dress, serving drinks at Neo on Clark Street. The bar was dark; there were no windows, only a blue-lit clock. Toni had thin caramel legs covered in track marks beneath his fishnet stockings. He brought me elegant-looking drinks on a silver tray. I hid in the corners or in the middle of the dance floor. I went to Neo alone and Toni sensed my loneliness and wanted to mother me to health but it didn't happen. Toni died at three in the morning in a stranger's apartment in Humboldt Park lying next to a broken needle, blood streaming from his nose, emerald skirt riding in waves across his hips, tights ripped, a slipper dangling from his toe, eyes wide open.

Then there was Toni's friend Tony. Tony worked at Berlin, had tribal tattoos covering half his body and long, thick black hair like a horse's mane, and every year the free weekly paper voted him best bartender in the city.

I had friends but they were sleeping, and they weren't real friends. Tony didn't charge me for drinks either and I hovered near his bar, an oasis next to the entrance. I danced close to Tony. I never wanted to go home. I said, "What kind of boys do you like?" and he said, "Straight boys," and I smiled.

Tony had a fashion show and I walked the runway in striped shorts with thin straps over my shoulders. There were so many people there, all of them high on pills, dehydrated and watching. I danced past them slowly. It was like being perfect, which is always an illusion. I was followed by a man in a straw hat, his gown covered in pale green bulbs. "Do you have any more swimsuits?" I asked Tony. "I want to go again."

"You are so vain," he said, patting my ass. I gave him a quick, sly kiss on the lips, before climbing back on the stage.

It was my stripper year. My heroin year. I danced Thursday nights at Berlin. Two sets, three songs, free whiskey, seventy-five dollars, occasional tips. They called me a go-go boy but really I was just decoration, cheap art. I scored heroin on the West Side, piloting my giant car through the burnt-out landscape, home of the '68 riots, the stained remnants of an assassination in Tennessee, the empty lots like broken teeth. Trash and parts everywhere, pipes protruding from the rubble, chassis on cinder blocks, men in lawn chairs on corners in front of vacant three-flats. I got robbed. I got beat up. Things weren't going well. Nothing made sense. I was having the best time of my life.

I didn't make enough money on a podium at Berlin. I danced at the Lucky Horseshoe, a front for prostitutes on Halsted Street. We weren't allowed to sit between sets. We had to mingle with clients at the bar. "They like it when you pay attention," the owner told us. "Open seats are for customers."

So we would stand and they would sit. I met a man who bred dogs. He stuck five dollars in my thong after my first dance. "It's like selling people," he said, laying a rough hand on my waist. "Only it's dogs, so it's legal." Then he let out a monstrous laugh.

The going rate was twenty dollars a day plus tips. The going rate was eighty dollars for a blowjob down at the Ram, a dirty theater with private booths six painted steps below street level a block away. There were sugar daddies that came to the Horseshoe but it was up to you to parse them from the fakers and dreamers. They said, "What do you want to do with your life? I can help you." If you were a writer they were an agent. If you were an actor they were a director, a producer. If you wanted to go to school they would give you a place to stay while you got your act together. They knew someone on the admissions board. The clients at the Horseshoe were whatever you might need. But I needed to be found attractive. I needed to be loved unconditionally. And I was very angry about something.

I had a college degree.

This is all true.

It was 1995, the hottest summer on record, or so somebody told me at the time. It's a fact I've never bothered to check. They were carrying dead seniors by the dozen in a phalanx of stretchers from the nursing homes on Touhy Avenue. I lived in a squat above a garage a bullet away from the project buildings. I could make out the top of the Sears Tower from my porch. I had a roommate and during the day we would go to the slab along North Avenue Beach and lie there like seals, diving into the water every twenty minutes or so until the sun went down. We'd lie on the concrete watching the sunset and then the stars. "Life is good," he said.

Sunday afternoons I danced between films at the Bijou. Twenty minutes of porn then one boy on the stage, one boy in the audience. The men pulled their penises out, stroking themselves, sliding a dollar in my pants with their free hands. The Bijou smelled of bleach. I climbed over the seats barefoot. I was like a spider, crawling along armrests and chair backs, never touching the ground. I stayed away from the older men. They had been around too long. They were looking for a good deal. I paid special attention to a fat boy who sat in the second row. He was probably my age and I felt sorry for him. He was so obese with all this skin falling around his face. His hair was flaxen and I worried that nobody loved him the most. I was projecting my own feelings. I sat on his lap, squeezed his shoulder, kissed his neck. I wanted to be capable of loving him for more than a few minutes but I wasn't. He gave me a dollar and I hugged him, pulling his nose against my naked chest. "It's OK," I said.

There were rooms above the Bijou. Offices, a movie studio. The manager kept a picture of me in his desk drawer. He asked me to act in a bisexual porn movie. I said I didn't mind. I was put in a room and given five minutes to get a hard-on. This was my audition. The room was giant and empty with slanted beams holding up the roof and great windows looking across Old Town. I jerked off, paging casually through the porn next to the bed. The director burst in with a Polaroid camera. "Yes," he exclaimed when he saw my hard-on.

The pay was three hundred dollars. I was told it was very important to be nice to the woman. She was a queen. I wanted the money but I was ambivalent about the film. What I really wanted was to be tied up. I wanted to be humiliated on tape. I wanted women with strap-ons to grip me by the throat and slide inside of me. I wanted to be wrapped in cellophane, like a present, unable to move. That was the kind of film I wanted to be in. But I didn't know how to say that at the time and people that don't know how to ask rarely get what they want.

I danced at the Manhole on lights out night. I was four feet above the floor on a square pedestal. I had to be careful not to step over the edge. Hands came from everywhere, palms stretching below my balls, fingers trying to find my asshole. I couldn't see past the elbows. "Stop it," I said softly. The music was so loud, nobody heard me.

It was my heroin year. I shot bags next to the couch and slept on the living room floor. I missed a night at Berlin. Then I missed another one. Summer was over. We stopped going to the beach. It got darker earlier. It was almost Thanksgiving. I dated Stacey, a Barbie-doll stripper with a bad coke habit and implants that didn't take; they felt like twelve-inch softballs inside her breasts. She made four hundred dollars a shift. She knew about bars in Cicero that never closed. She crashed her car and the barmaid asked if she spilled her drink. Her other boyfriend was a police officer. "He's very violent," she told me. "He wants to put his gun in your mouth and ask you some questions. He broke the lock on my door. Do you want to come over?"

After Stacey I dated Zahava. Zahava came from a good southern family. She had been a pom-pom girl. She had been to finishing school. It seemed like she was always happy. She was the only person I knew with good posture. She wanted me to go to law school. I turned her on to heroin. Years later she would tell me I was the first bad thing that ever happened to her.

Zahava said I was handsome. I told her when you're a stripper you don't worry about your appearance. You always feel attractive when people are willing to pay to see you naked. It was the biggest lie I ever told. I stared at the other strippers, the bricks in their stomachs, trapezoids like baby mountains. It made me nauseous to think about. I wasn't good enough looking to dance at the Vortex but they let me in for free. I was low-rent and I knew it. I had an eating disorder and long hair. The only advantage I had over anybody was that I knew how to dance.

I was in a small room with dark wood floors on top of a big house in Evanston near the lake when I took a hotshot and passed out with blood streaming from my nose and foam gurgling at my mouth. Just like Toni a year earlier. My friend turned me over so I wouldn't choke on my own vomit, then he left me to die.

But I didn't die. Firemen came the next day. They were strong and good. They strapped me to a chair, carried me down three flights of stairs. "Where's your family?" the owner of the house asked as they hauled me past her. "What's your parents' phone number?" I didn't tell her. It was the first good decision I made that year. I was paralyzed for eight days and the nurses let me piss all over myself.

"I can't move," I told them.

"You can move," they replied.

When I was discharged from the hospital I walked with a limp. I told people I fell down a flight of stairs. Eventually the limp went away but it took time. And it took time to learn how to eat. I lost thirty pounds.

I didn't strip again. Or shoot heroin. I got a master's degree. I moved to a ski resort. Like all the other employees I wore black pants, a white shirt, and a patterned vest. We looked like dancing monkeys. Every day someone would stare at the mountains while I refilled their cup. "I wish I could trade places with you," they would say, maybe dropping a dollar into the pitcher sitting empty on the counter's edge, then stepping outside and disappearing down the hill.

What It's Like in San Francisco

I WAS LIVING IN A WHITE FORD FIESTA with a blue stripe along the doors, parked on top of a hill above the Castro District, wheels lodged against the curb. I had a blanket—a present from my ex-fiancée—a bicycle, a bag of clothes, and a few boxes of paper that I thought represented something important stuffed below the windowpane. And in retrospect I realize they did, but not what I thought.

I'd only been in San Francisco a couple of days. I had run out of gas on the Oakland side of the Bay Bridge on the way into town and the emergency worker who showed up in a big padded truck asked me if I had a death wish. I could barely hear him with the wind so loud and the cars racing over the bay. I had to yell to explain that the gas gauge was broken, that I usually got three hundred miles to the tank, but this tank had only gotten two hundred and fifty for some reason. He pushed me onto Treasure Island and injected my car with an electric pump, which forced a quart of gas straight through the hoses and into the engine. I'd been driving aimlessly in the desert for weeks and hadn't had a conversation in what seemed like a long time.

San Francisco was beautiful and full of fog as the ocean air drifted across the city. It was nearly summer. Tufts of cloud hung on the edges of the Peaks like cotton caught on a drainpipe. The fog made the colors pop and the rows of pink and green pastel houses lining the hills had the quality of a painting, like something too perfect to have happened by accident. Nothing felt real and I wondered if I would stay once I found a job for a bit and made some money. I was running out of places to go. I'd been traveling for a long time and forgotten why.

I went to a poetry reading and I met a poet there, Diana, with braided black hair dyed in streaks of orange and pink. She was taller than me by four inches with a broad, strong back, and her poems were the angry poems of a victim returning home with a box of matches and a can of lighter fluid. Her anger was ravenous and her words mixed with sadness and self-loathing that ran straight to the bone. In her combat boots, motorcycle jacket, and tar-stained jeans, I thought she was beautiful.

It was late on a Sunday and there weren't many people in the sharply lit windows of the busses and trolleys clattering down Market Street past the grocery and the taqueria. After the reading we found our way to a punk rock bar with a solid jukebox full of Pixies and Ramones, and several rows of hard wood tabletops and tall stools. There were five or six people bellied up to the rail, which is where we sat as well. The bar was not well lit, but there was enough light to see by.

Diana let me know she was living with her girlfriend and would be still for a long time. She presented this to me defiantly, like it would change my mind about something. But I didn't care. It was six months since I'd left my fiancée. Diana said she had been an editor for a big magazine but now she was unemployed and taking pills. I told her I had won a poetry slam back in Chicago. We were both dissatisfied with our current predicaments, not because they were bad, but because they were insulting. We were better than the world was willing to admit. I asked her if she wanted to add a shot to her beer and she said she did.

After a few drinks I slid my hand between her legs. Not inside her jeans, outside, rubbing the denim seam with the bridge of my hand, forcing her zipper against her pelvis. "Oh, we're doing that," she said, and unzipped my pants and pulled my penis out and started stroking me below the bar. The bartender looked over at us once then looked away. She gripped me tightly and pulled, letting her thumbnail scratch the tip of my penis. I thought she was going to tear my skin. I was so lonely I laid my head on her cold leather shoulder.

I thought, Yes, this is San Francisco. Before San Francisco I'd spent twelve hours in the shade of the post office on a park bench in Moab, Utah, unable to move. Before that I spent four months as a ski bum in the Rocky Mountains, at one of those giant outdoor athletic parks where the men outnumber the women seven to one. I was fresh out of a two-and-a-half-year relationship that had broken everything inside of me, and I was still running from that.

I kept a hand on my drink. She yanked my belt buckle and unbuttoned my pants, forced her large hand down further around my balls, and gave a quick, solid squeeze. I let out a cry and pressed my face into her hair, but nobody seemed to care. I zipped back up and left my empty glass as I followed her drunkenly, belt still undone, into the ladies' room.

What I loved the most about her was her size. She was proportionally Amazon, thin but with enormous breasts, wide hips, and Marine shoulders. She was so much bigger than me it was like she could fit me in her pocket.

She forced me up against the back of the stall, her forearm on my neck, her hand inside my shirt, and she kissed me hard. "What do you want?" she asked, pulling away and yanking my shirt over my head.

"Hit me," I said. Or I might have said "Hurt me" or something else. But whatever I said was lost in the fabric; she didn't hear me right. She thought I said,

"Choke me," and gripped my throat and squeezed my windpipe shut. My breath was gone and I saw stars and she pulled on me frantically. "Come on," she said. "C'mon. C'mon." I felt my legs go as the screws and beams rattled in their bearings and then I came all over the stall.

I was lying on the cool pink bathroom floor and she was sitting on the toilet, her pants bunched over her boots. I ran my fingers gently across her laces while she peed. The bathroom door opened and closed several times but nobody said anything. That's the kind of city San Francisco is.

"I want to see you again," I said. It was easy for me. I didn't know anyone and I had nothing to lose.

She snatched sheets of toilet paper and rubbed them quickly between her legs. She looked down on me with something resembling guilt, but not quite, rather the realization of two ideas that don't exactly contradict but affect and enhance each other. She didn't like me anymore. I was desperate and lost and she had problems of her own.

"Usually, I'm a lesbian," she said looking away, flushing the toilet.

I didn't know yet that I would stay in San Francisco for nine years and see her many more times and we'd become friends but not lovers and one winter day, on our way to catch some acquaintances at a party, she would ask me to wait with her outside the building then force her entire fist into my mouth. At the time, on the bathroom floor, I was pretty sure I wouldn't meet her again. I didn't know where I'd be. I leaned toward the tip of her boot, sniffing the old leather of her shoe.

My Girlfriend Comes to the City and Beats Me Up

MY GIRLFRIEND, who I met on one of those online boards for "kinky" people, came to the city and I met her at the train station and we went to eat. We went to a fancy restaurant and she paid. She doesn't want to be in debt to me in any way. Then we had a couple of drinks at a bar near my house where I ran into some friends. I asked her on the way to my apartment, "What do you want me to do when we get inside." And she said, "I'll decide that, maybe I want it to be a surprise."

Inside the apartment she acted angry. "Why don't you just tell me my scene? Why don't you do that? Any more suggestions?" She slapped me across the face with every question. I shook my head and said I was sorry. "It's too late for sorry."

The problem was, she had done this already. It's a setup. If I don't say anything she gets upset by my quiet. If I do say something she uses it against me. She always starts with this angry thing and I knew she was just creating something to be angry about. This was the first time I knew for sure she wasn't really angry, or not angry about something specific, just a general rage. It was a moment of insight; she was faking it. And I decided that I would make it through this and I would be OK and I would never see her again. She slapped me hard, on the side of my face, and my ear began to ring loudly, and I thought that this was another reason I wouldn't see her again, because of health concerns.

"Don't you dare leave town again without my permission. You think this is just a scene, but it's not. I mean it."

Some of the usual stuff followed. She stripped me naked and kept her own clothes on. She gave me a hard spanking. She grabbed my hair and banged my head into the floor several times. I don't have the equipment she has. At her house she has bolts in the wall to hang chains from and thousands of dollars' worth of expensive masks, strap-ons, sharpie disposal kits, and cuffs and gags. I wasn't tied up. I could fight back, but I didn't. I just wanted to wait it out. I had looked forward to seeing her. I had been on the East Coast for two weeks. We hadn't seen each other for three. And now I regretted it. All of it. And I questioned what had led me to this particular moment in the first place. It wasn't like we had anything to talk about. It's not like outside of the bedroom we had interesting conversations or anything. She was hurting me and being mean and it was so unreasonable. Maybe if I was tied up or something I could get in the mood. But what do you do when you're not in the mood and someone is hitting you and you want them to stop? She pushed her fist against my eye socket a couple of times and threatened me with a black eye.

She was straddling me in her blue jeans when she said, "I'm not your father." She was still angry about something I had suggested, or that I had hurried her out of the bar and she hadn't finished her drink. It was all made up. A game. But I started to feel sad when she mentioned my father. I have such an awful relationship with my father. Aren't you supposed to forgive and forget stuff? I was thirteen when I left home. It's been seventeen years since he caught me and beat me and shaved my head and the state took custody and I became a ward of the court. We try to mend things but I get these letters from him and it's just too much. He thinks *he's* the victim. Like I have victimized him by making him out to be such a horrible father. But he was a horrible father and I spent a year, a full year, sleeping on rooftops and in hallways and eating out of garbage cans and all he remembers are the times I came home to shower, proof that I didn't have it so bad. I was only thirteen, then fourteen...

Then she says, still staring down at me with such contempt, my arms pinned beneath her knees, her hands balled into fists, "I'm not your mother reincarnate." And I'm thinking why would she say that? Who would say such a god-awful thing? I'm staring up between her denim legs, and she's been slapping me so much that the side of my face is swollen. Try to imagine this, the feeling of her thighs, a chinese printed top made from expensive silk; I can just barely make out her breasts. Her angry face, which is long and oval like an egg that's been stretched but hasn't broken. A hardwood floor. She's so angry and I shake my head just a little and start to cry.

At first it's a tiny muffled cry, a small something that comes out. And I'm asking myself, even in my own head where I always watch things from the distance, I'm wondering where on earth did that come from? She'll leave soon, take the train home, and I won't see her again. I mean, she's already gone too far so many times. She's cut me with scalpels and pierced me. I'm not allowed to wear clothes in her house or sit on the furniture. She embarrasses me in public. I didn't check the box that said 24/7. I didn't sign up for this kind of lifestyle. I didn't want this. But I don't know what I want, I never have. And she's always been honest with me, and I've done nothing but lie to her. Then I'm crying more, and soon I can't stop crying.

"It's OK," she says. But it's not OK. What kind of a person would say something so awful, *I'm not your mother reincarnate*. It's unimaginable. I feel limp, like

I have no bones. And she's standing and pulling me with
her to the couch where she sits and I'm kneeling in front
of her with my face in her lap. "I'm not going anywhere,"
she says. And she strokes my face and this makes me
think she is going to hit me again so I'm crying harder.
And soon I'm on the couch with her, curled around her
waist, over her lap, still crying. I'm apologizing. I really
want to stop crying but I can't. "This is the place to let
it out," she says, like she's a therapist. Like this is
healthy or something. And then this time comes where
I start to ask her to hurt me. I say it in this small, child-
like voice, because I feel like a small child.

"Please."

"Please what?"

"Please hurt me."

Why do I want her to hurt me now? Now that I feel
so vulnerable and sad. But she's not saying mean things
anymore. She's pinching me hard in places, my nipples,
so hard I scream. "Beg," she says. And I do. "Please don't
stop," I say, my voice getting higher and softer the more
she squeezes, the more it hurts, until I'm certain she'll
break the skin. Why do I like it now and not before? It
hurts so much. "I want you to cut me again," I whisper
into the pillow, curled around her. I'm her baby. "I want
you to carve your initials on me. And I want you to
pierce me."

"You didn't like it at the time," she says.

"I did like it. I just didn't know how to respond."

She promises. She says next time I come to see her at her home she will dig her initials into my back.

She keeps going. Spanking me really hard, tying up my penis and balls, dragging me around the apartment by my hair. And it's hours later when we go to sleep and she's missed her train home.

I sleep on the inside of the spoon. She's my abusive boyfriend and I feel safe, her arms wrapped around me. She looks wonderful in her underwear. Her skin is warm, brown, and smooth. She smells so good. In the morning I don't want her to leave. I slide my face between her naked legs. She opens her eyes and looks down on me. It's only six and the alarm will ring soon. "What do you think you're doing?" But she doesn't make me move. She grabs my hair and closes her eyes.

I take a taxi with her to the train station for the seven a.m. The first time she came to the city I had also accompanied her to the train station. And before her train came she grabbed me roughly by my vest and pulled me to the other side of the station where she kissed me. That was our first moment of intimacy. That was a long time ago.

It's a bright day and her train has gone and I'm filled with hunger. I feel like I could eat three meals. It's always been hard for me to imagine that there are others like me out there, healthy couples who tie each other up and beat each other with belts and then go to the movies or something. And of course there are other people like me, lots of them. You can judge it by the size of the BDSM section on the porn store walls and all the videos and books they carry even in regular bookstores. All of those books seem to have the same message, that it's OK. I despise that message. Sure, you have to live. And of course, if there are people like me, a normal enough guy who wants to be hurt, who fantasizes at night about an anonymous woman running a razor the length of his body and cutting him open, then there exists the opposite of me. Women like her. She wrote me a letter while I was in Washington, DC. She said what she'd really like to do, in her fantasy, is beat me way past the point of crying, to the point of yelling Oh Please God No, and the neighbors wouldn't come. Nobody would come. She wanted to hit me across my back with a chain. But still, even as I'm missing her, and knowing that I will see her again, the question stays with me. The idea of two people finding each other. A person who wants to be hurt and another who wants to hurt someone. We've never had sex. We won't have sex. I've never even seen her naked. I just don't understand where it comes from that some-one could say such a thing.

Other Desires

JUST PROMISE ME your devotion.

Sometimes when my phone rings I try to hide in my own apartment. I close the blinds. The phone rings in the front of the studio near the window and I crawl toward the end of my mattress, where the walls meet. While the phone rings I push into the corner and the sheets slide beneath my feet and then the mattress and I'm lying on the wood floor staring into the ceiling, its web of thick steel beams and spotted white plaster. And when the phone stops ringing I go to check who it is. It's always her.

Early in the morning before I leave for work, I press the PLAY button on the answering machine. Ambellina's thick, steady voice wakes me.

Understand that this decision was hastened by the feeling I get that you need someone to offer protection, love, and discipline. I know that you're afraid. But I will keep you safe. Honesty is so important in this relationship. I don't do things in halves. You can call me when you feel jealous, uncertain, or insecure. Please arrange to meet me on Saturday. You can lay your head in my lap then.

"Any letters from your girlfriend?" Valerie asks. It's 6:45 in the morning. I have a headache. I hate myself. We're on the two Internet kiosks in the front of the store. The small round tables have all been wiped down and the blue rags thrown in the sink. The newspapers are stacked beneath the advertisements taped to the wall next to the coffee lids. The bagels are sitting in baskets on three slanted shelves behind the glass.

"Shut up," I say. "Put on the coffee." Valerie has pink hair and she likes to get high. We've worked together in this bagel shop for three years now. This is the question she always asks and this is the answer I always give her, to get up, to change the cauldrons, to unbolt the front door and invite in another working day.

Valerie bounces to Sly and the Family Stone as our first customers arrive, spinning around the large square cutting block. "Do you think it's better to play bass or drums?" she asks. "Because if you play bass then you're in front and everybody sees you. But if you play drums you stay in shape and let out all that anger."

"Bass," I tell her.

The first orders are to-go orders, toasted rolls, egg bagels with dill cream cheese, tall coffees and lattes for people scrambling to trains. Later, people start to sit down. We put the tubs back in the refrigerator. Valerie switches the music to '80s new wave. "Such a wonderful problem," she sings, raising her fists over her head, swinging them forward from her elbows. "Oh please let me help you."

There are two rooms in the shop and a thin hallway between them. The workers, students, and professionals sit in front near the windows. The junkies and the criminals sit in the back. We let them. They hang out by the fire exit and the restroom with the hookers from Folsom Street who break into the bins in front of the chocolate factory at night. The prison bus stops only two blocks away. The dealers hang out on 16th Street and two doors down in the shooting gallery. I stare at them while pouring the beans into the grinder. The click of the phone. The cauldrons lean forward. The whir of the machine crushing the beans. The tap of the espresso filter. The junkies nod toward the Formica. Valerie's boyfriend, Philc, hangs back there with them, juggling ketchup packets, mini-hypodermics hanging from his ears, wearing a thick spiked collar around his neck. He's always dirty. He likes to brag about his skills with a knife. He says he was a knife thrower with the circus. He sleeps in the shopping cart encampment under the overpass. He steals from the junkies when they sleep.

Bell comes to my apartment at eight p.m. She makes me nervous and shy. I've washed the smell of coffee and lox from my hair, cleaned beneath my nails. I've changed clothes. There's a bowl of caramel popcorn on the table because that's what she likes.

"My husband knows," she says. She walks deliberately, one boot in front of the other. "Yeah, I told him."

She sits on the couch, leans forward first with her fists on her knees and then leans back as I assume my position. She's eating the popcorn. She's drinking white wine from my only glass. Between the small couch and the table I am on the floor on my knees with my head in her lap. "You don't mind, do you? That he knows?" I shake my head, rub my cheek on the fabric of her skirt; feel her fingers moving on my head, deciding what they are going to do. There is only one way she wants the question to be answered. She wants me to be jealous and yanks my head by my hair. I breathe heavily when her grip tightens and she twists her knuckles, sending small pins of pain along my skull. My mouth opens.

"What?" she asks. She slaps me. "What do you want to say?" She lets go of my hair and reclines. I stare into her chest, the lines on the country of her body.

"My husband doesn't want you to see these." She pushes her breasts together with her forearms. "That's what he asked. These are his favorite." She puckers her lips. She's wearing a thin black negligee. When she's not holding them her breasts slide toward her elbows. They are big, but not firm. More importantly, I don't care about her husband.

"Look at me," she says. "Look at me." Bell has a broad face and a wide, flat nose; clipped curly hair dyed maroon. "You're pouting." I nod. "Didn't I tell you I would protect you? What are you so worried about?" Her hands are large. Everything about her is large. I close my eyes then the slaps come, back and forth, until I cry, and still more. "Shutup," she hisses. "Shutup. Don't cry. Don't cry. You're mine. Don't cry." And when she stops and her hand slides away from my face I lower my head. I duck carefully toward her. I try to burrow into her, under her skirt, to be inside of her. It's still early. There will be hours more of this. And I will pretend to be jealous of her husband, who may or may not exist. Because it's important to her that I be jealous, so I am, because she likes it.

I met Bell two weeks ago on one of those online personals boards for people with other desires. Places filled with leather-clad professionals who charge more for an hour than I make in a week, and lonely housewives who say they want to *try something new*. The boards use black backgrounds and are suggestive of something wild. A whip hangs in the left corner of the screen. They give you a form to fill out when you join. They ask you what you're into: Eurologia (piss play), Collar and Lead, Smothering, Vibrators, Pain,

Asphyxiaphilia (breath play), Amputees, Electrotorture, Fisting, Tongues, Ears, Feet, Cross-Dressing, Humiliation, 24/7, Cling Film, Erotic Email Exchange, Cock and Ball Torture. The list goes on and on. They ask your role: dominant, submissive, switch. They ask how often you think about the lifestyle. Twice a week they send you Love Dog Reports. It's all angles, women next to punching bags, free pornographic sites that aren't free. Everybody wants to know your real email so they can put you on their list. It's mostly men using the site. There are discussion boards and the men's names are blue and the women's pink and couples are green, but even the women are most likely men. And then Bell, who posted no picture and whose ad read *East Bay Woman looking for a toy to abuse. Must be full-time. No equivocating.* And I responded by saying I would be her toy, full-time. I sent her a picture. I said that she would be my only commitment and I didn't think she would respond but she did.

And the bookstores with all of their trade paperbacks and Eric Stanton artwork saying that it's OK to be weird, to accept who we are. It's fun, they say, to play during sex. To tie each other up and take control. It's just sex. It's just a game. Trade places, let off some steam.

I was raped the first time by a middle-aged caseworker in a small green room in the Chicago Juvenile Detention Facility. The windows were closed and the room was dusty and hot and filled with stacks of yellowing, creased paper forced into wide brown envelopes. Mr. Gracie didn't ask me if it was OK and he didn't apologize afterward. When I masturbate at night I think of him, not of his image or his malty smell, just the darkness and the fear and the pain. I've never stopped fantasizing about it, replaying it in my mind. And that's what I think about when Bell buckles into her strap-on and pushes me over the table, her thick hand around my neck closing my windpipe, the weight of her wide hips pressing against me. It hurts. "Poor Theo," she says, her nails tearing across my back. "My little Tolstoy. You just want to hide here." And I nod because when I don't nod the beatings will start again.

The fog is pouring over Twin Peaks, through the Castro and into the Mission. It tumbles down the hillside blanketing the small white houses. It was so warm the other day. When the fog pushes in the valley gets cold. In Chicago the buildings are mountains but here the hills are real. The wind cuts down the streets. In a few hours the city will be grey. They're running elections for District Supervisor and the streets are peppered in slogans. Daly for Tenants' Rights. Cheng for Change. Men are selling paperbacks next to Macondo and the Kilowatt. The cardboard placards fly down the street. I'm standing at a pay phone next to the movie theater, across from the Copy King where I pick up my mail. It's five o'clock. People are stepping off and onto trains, getting home from work.

I hold my collar tight around my neck. "I can't meet you," Bell says. She does this. She cancels on me a lot. She wants to know what I'm wearing. She wants to talk sexy. "Get me off," she says. "Imagine me hitting you. Imagine the phone between my legs. I'm sitting on your face. I'm smothering you. You can't breathe."

"I'm on a pay phone," I say. "People can see me."

"Are you ashamed?" she asks.

"Yes," I respond.

"That's your problem. Have Friday open for me."

"Bell, I can't."

"You what?"

"I have to work."

A bus has stopped in front of me and the driver is out in the street pulling frantically on the cables, his passengers staring through the windows, an old Chinese woman stuck at the rear door trying to get off.

"Do you know how many submissives answered my ad?" She waits for my answer. "Do you know how many men there are like you, who want a strong woman to keep them in place? Do you think you're the only one I could have? There's thousands of men like you. I get letters every day."

"I'm sorry."

"Do you think I care about that?" she asks. There's a long pause, like she's considering what to say next.

"Listen. You will see me when I want to see you. You will make time for me when I tell you to. You will," she says. "You will." Then she hangs up on me. I place my fingers against my forehead and try to block out the sounds of the city, the shoes on the pavement and the running sewers. I lean against the Currency Exchange, next to a street vender selling old magazines, and sit down for a second on the sidewalk.

Valerie is running from the cauldrons to the toaster, a bright, pink flash of light. I take over the espresso machine and she shoves a square tub of peanut butter forward and I grab it before it smacks the side of the machine. "Back so soon?" she asks. One click, one shot. Two clicks. Bagels at the toaster. Jam. Cream cheese.

"I'm taking a cigarette break," Valerie says. She stands in the fire exit with a cigarette looking back at the counter to make sure a line doesn't form. There's never been a fire here. She's thirty-five and twice divorced. She dresses like a schoolgirl with her pink pigtails but the creases around her mouth and her eyes give her away. She wears turquoise panty hose intentionally torn at the calf. I slice three sections of onion and stick my hand into the caper bin. We used to go to concerts together before Philc started coming around. Now she has one arm crossed over her chest holding her elbow. Philc has a small BMX bike as high as my knees and he is standing on the front wheel of it now, bouncing near the muffin boxes. "Check this out," he says to Valerie, swinging the little bicycle under his leg.

"That's so good, Philc."

I think I expressly said I was looking for a sub in my ad. If you are now my sub, then by definition I am your Mistress. Please address me accordingly.

Forget about Friday if it is such a hassle. I shall see you in a few weeks.

Pat owns a string of bagel shops but this one was his first. They used to make the bagels next door but now that's a photo studio and the bagels are baked in a warehouse near Potrero Hill. The store was opened in the '60s, a gathering spot for protestors. We have a news article framed on the wall above the ATM and it's got a picture of a young Pat on a stage speaking to an enormous crowd on a grass lawn with university buildings in the background. The headline reads, *Students say, Not Our War!* He comes in while we're closing. He likes to tell us stories of San Francisco's past. "You used to get a lid of grass for twenty dollars. You could have sex with a thirteen-year-old girl and when her mom asked about it you did her too."

"I doubt it," Valerie says.

I lock the door for the night and Pat sparks a joint. I take a hit and hand it to Valerie. We're tired. We've been on our feet all day.

"Yeah, well. I exaggerate sometimes. Keeps life interesting." Pat folds his hands across his large stomach and lets out a sigh. Valerie's laugh is like a birdsong. "I ought to start drug testing you guys. If it's OK with Clinton that makes it unanimous. Fucking Reagan. Here's your war on drugs." Pat takes a long toke and leans his head back, smoke gurgling out between his lips and dribbling up his face. A sixty-year-old hippie in a tie-dyed shirt and blue jeans. He's probably worth a million bucks.

Report in immediately. I'm waiting.

At the Dress for Less I tell the saleslady I'm buying underwear for my girlfriend and she asks me what size my girlfriend is and I say, "Oh, she's about my size."

The apartment's never clean enough for Bell. I don't own very much but what I have lacks character. It's just white space. I live on the third floor and dust seems to collect from the windows. I have new dust every day. She told me to prepare her something to eat so I bought chicken breasts and spinach at the Bi-Rite and they're ready for her but she doesn't seem hungry. "Did you get any wine?" I pour her a glass of wine. Hand it to her. Kneel down in front of her. She smells thick, like milk and brown sugar. "Amuse me," she says. I look around my own apartment. It's a foreign place. There is nothing here. I have a small television on a short, dark stand. No computer. I have a Monopoly game, a table, a mattress, a small couch, a phone, an answering machine with blue buttons. I don't even know how I amuse myself. "Are you trying to manipulate me?" Bell asks. "Is this what I want or what you want?"

I flinch when Ambellina raises her hand. I close my eyes and wait. At Prairie View they said I had a twitch. Out in the woods by the border of Wisconsin with other bad children, miles from the nearest hitchhiking road, surrounded by big brown trees, trunks as thick as truck tires. All the doors are locked and you have to ask permission just to use the bathroom. They run it on a point system. Henry Horner Children's Adolescent Center on the grounds of Reed Mental Hospital uses time-out rooms and drugged Kool-Aid, and straps you to a bed when things get out of hand. Thorazine was big for kids in the '80s. They never let you speak in court. They keep logbooks full of your flaws. Pass notes about you back and forth, from social worker to caseworker to therapist to hospital intern. They never let you read what they've written.

I want to tell Ambellina something, but I don't trust her. She squeezes the handcuffs closed on my wrists. She also has a blindfold, which she wraps over my eyes. She runs tape over my mouth and I start to shake my head no and scream but it's just muffled and she's telling me to shut up again but I can't. I knock into the wall. Bang my head against the wall. Everything inside of me is black and rushing forward stopping in front of that big wad of tape. She pins me with her leg while she chains my ankles. I'm telling myself not to scream but as I struggle the handcuffs get tighter, cutting the circulation to my wrists. I keep screaming these strange, muffled sounds into the tape. I can't control myself. My mouth fills with glue. And she's slapping me and then punching me. "Stop it," she says, reaching between my legs, squeezing hard, her other fist landing against my eye. "Stop it." It's like glass, like a car crash, like falling out of a plane.

I'm on the floor and Bell is on the mattress, my face between her legs when she rips the tape off my mouth. I feel the skin of her thighs. It feels warm and it feels like it is everywhere around me and I'm floating and breathing somehow in this dark pool. "Do you want me to take the blindfold off?" she asks and I whisper, *no.* But it hardly comes out so I shake my head no and she touches my hair. I'm damp. I feel her body moving around me and the dark room. I feel safe. She says something about her child. A girl. She sounds sad but I can't make out what she's saying. Something about her husband and her child. She's very sad about something.

In the morning Valerie has a black eye and I do too. She's stacking plates. I heft a forty-pound sack of beans from beneath the counter. Somebody knocks on the door and then runs away. We're still closed. My body hurts and I feel like I will never get better.

"I don't want to talk about it," Valerie says. Valerie's black eye extends down her cheekbones where it becomes yellow. She shakes her head.

It's seven o'clock. We're done setting up. Neither of us makes a move to open the door. A lady in black pants, a white shirt, and a blazer is knocking. Valerie stares at her but doesn't do anything. Valerie shouldn't worry. This is our cafe. I pull out a rag and rub down the display case. The lady knocks harder and pulls on the handle, *cack cack cack,* as the deadbolt rattles through the plate glass. "She doesn't need any coffee," I say. "She's already awake."

But Valerie goes to the door and lets the woman in. The woman has a tight face that pulls forward to the tip of her nose, her skin stretched over the hollows of her cheeks, her mouth small and circular. She looks from Valerie to me, sees our black eyes, and decides not to say anything more than "One large coffee please." She looks at her thin, gold watch. "I'm late," she says helplessly.

The lady leaves but more people follow and Valerie and I run back and forth, turning the crank that keeps the shop operating. The junkies fill up the back room. We pour old espresso into the ice coffee jug, stack orange juice and mini-containers full of lox spread and white-fish salad. Philc comes in at some point. He pushes the girl with the tattooed face who is on the nod at the table near the dishbin. "Get up," he says. "You owe me a soup packet." She doesn't answer and he says, "I'll cut you." He's rummaging through her bags, a black garbage bag and a Barbie doll lunchbox.

"Theo."

A line of customers is forming in the front of the store. But I'm watching Philc and when he realizes I'm watching him and that Valerie is watching him he jumps up and spreads his arms in the middle of the floor.

"Ta-da!" he says. He does a dance step where he walks a perfect square. Then he tries to walk behind the counter but I stop him with the broom.

"You can't come back here. You don't work here."

"What are you doing?" he asks me, his face turning red, throwing his hand slightly forward and spreading his fingers, like he is letting go of something and I should be wary.

"What are you doing?" Valerie asks.

"He doesn't belong behind the counter," I say to Valerie and her black eye and back to Philc, who is looking at the floor now and rummaging in his jacket pocket for the handle to something.

I poke Philc in the sternum with the broom. A small man with sand-colored dreadlocks behind him says, "Say, man. Could you buzz me into the bathroom?"

"You think you could take me, bro?" Philc asks, turning his head ninety degrees into his shoulder, crunching his ear against his collarbone, then walking away from me, slapping a fist into his palm. He walks straight back to the emergency exit muttering, "You think you could take me?"

Philc kicks open the emergency exit. It opens to a small yard filled with garbage and recycling.

"C'mon," Philc says, standing next to the bathroom door, biting at his lips.

"Get out of here."

"You're not part of this," he tells me. He raises his boot and lowers it as hard as he can onto the foot of the girl with the tattooed face and she wakes with a loud scream and falls to the floor holding her foot. Philc pulls a rock out, whips it past my shoulder and a bottle of syrup breaks. He runs up and puts a foot into the glass display case.

"You don't belong here."

"You don't belong here," he answers me back as the front door closes behind him. The girl in the back has curled into a ball and is making small, high-pitched noises. Glass and syrup are everywhere. It's just glass and syrup but I don't know what to do about it.

I look over at Valerie and she's crying so hard she's choking. She looks like a mermaid—her pink hair, all those tears.

We've closed up. Pat is coming to look at the damage. Pat knows, with all of his talk of revolution, this is junkie central. The cost of doing business. I'm cleaning up the glass and mopping the syrup. There's glass in the bagels so I throw all of the bagels away. Valerie straightens the countertop, dumps out the coffee that's getting old and starting to burn, fastens the cap on the purple onions sliced from this morning. Picks up the pastries and throws them away.

"That's where you get that black eye," Valerie says. "You like to fight. You like to pick fights. You like to pick fights with people's boyfriends." She's still puffy faced and red. I make an espresso because I suddenly feel tired.

"No," I say. "That's not how I got this."

"Fuck you, Theo," she says. "Fuck you and your problems."

I'm wearing women's underwear and leather pants at the 16th Street BART station, worried that someone will see me, when Bell gets off the train. We walk back three blocks to my apartment, past the liquor stores and the transient hotels. Men with blankets on their shoulders huddle between doorways next to the Quick Mart. "You should have gotten me a cab," she says. There's been a fire in the red building on Van Ness. It was a single resident occupancy and spray-painted on the brick is DEATH TO LANDLORDS. "I'm in marriage counseling. You didn't know that." Bell pulls out a cigarette. She never smoked before. She shakes her head. I almost tell her that I was married once. How I got thrown out of the abortion clinic downtown. But I think better of it, because she'd want to know why, or she wouldn't want to know at all.

And anyway years have passed. And this is today. "I have a daughter." She hands me her lighter and when I light her cigarette for her she blows the smoke in my face. "Yesterday, in front of our counselor, I told my husband I was leaving him." She stops and I stop with her. She doesn't even seem to care that I almost kept walking. "What do you think will happen to my little girl? Answer," she says. We're in front of my building.

"We should go inside," I suggest.

"You can do better than that."

"Bell, I don't know anything about children."

"Open this damn door," she says.

I make her a cup of coffee. She stands by the window peering cautiously through the blinds to the street. I crawl to her on my knees. She looks down at me skeptically. "You couldn't give me what I want in a million years," she says. She places her leg on a chair and guides my face to her and tells me where to lick and where to suck. "That's where my husband fucks me," she says. I'm stretching my neck as she lifts beneath my chin, surrounded by her legs. "Stop," she says, pushing me away. Stripping her top and skirt. She's getting fat. "Do you think I'm the most beautiful woman?"

"I do," I say. We're going through the motions. The next forty minutes is spent with me trying to please her with my tongue until my mouth is dry and sore.

She slaps me a few times over by the couch and for a moment I think this is going to work. She hits me particularly hard once and I feel my eye starting to swell again and she stops. "Lie down on the bed," she says. "My husband doesn't want me to do this." She slides over me. Of course I'm not wearing protection. Nothing is safe. She rides up over me. Like an oven. She says, "Theo, darling." She grabs my hands and places them on her thighs. She lies on top of me, biting me lightly. I grip her legs and stay quiet. Her chest against my chest. This is sex. There's no real threat. If I yell loud enough she'll stop, which leaves us with nothing. And when I say I exist only to please her I don't mean it. And when she tells me how beautiful she is it's because she doesn't believe it. Or when she says she has to punish me and asks me if I'm scared, she doesn't mean it. We don't mean it.

Bell is wrapping a belt around her skirt. I turn away from her and watch the door. "My husband would like to see me with you. He wants to see me with a submissive. Then he'll realize it's not a threat to him. Because of course you are not. Then, when I'm done with you, he'll make love to me like a real man. We'll discuss it first. I want you to come over, to the East Bay."

I walk her down the stairs, past the bicycles locked to the stairwell and onto the Mission streets. Bell gets in the cab and I give the driver my money. "Take her to Oakland," I tell him. "She has to meet her husband."

"I'll see you on Tuesday," Bell says.

"I love you," I tell her back.

Pat and I meet at the Uptown on 17th Street. A holdover from the revolution. The walls are covered with slogans for left-wing political movements. The tables are carved and stickered. There are two red couches in the back, a jukebox and a pool table. A view of the hookers who walk by at street level. Pat orders us two speakeasies and two shots of whiskey and he pays for them. He always pays for the drinks and we never talk about it. He starts like he always does. "In the '60s," he says, drinking his beer, "we were trying to change society."

"So much for that idea," I tell him.

"You'd be amazed how much fun you can have if you get out of your own head. The problem is that now people are only interested in themselves. What we have is a nonvoting generation. That's what they should call you guys, the nonvoting generation. You think you can't fix anything until you fix yourselves. Well, let me be the first to tell you, you will never fix yourself."

Somebody throws some money into the jukebox at the same time a rack of pool balls slam into the gully. The Pixies, *I will grow, up to be, a debaser.*

"My wife," I tell Pat. "I didn't always sell bagels."

"What about your wife?"

"Oh man. She was a sweetheart. Long legs, black hair. When people met her they said she had breeding. Because she walked so straight. But you know, she didn't. I mean, we didn't always get along. Like, we didn't agree on a lot of things. We hated each other. She wanted things from me. I felt like I could never give them to her."

Pat's looking in his whiskey glass with one eye, waiting for me to finish. I know all about Pat's marriage. His childhood sweetheart. And how her head isn't right anymore. "So what's wrong with selling bagels?"

"Nothing wrong with it." I drink my beer. Pat's good for at least one more round. Maybe two. A perk of the job, I suppose, but still I'm the one who has to be up at six in the morning. I only live two blocks away from this bar. I come here often. When the phone is ringing. When the fog is falling over the hills. I sit here at night with a beer, not trying to get drunk, just trying to make it last. Staring into the wall and the liquor bottles, the mirror. The mirror is rounded with a dark wood edge barreled around it. I like to watch the young couples that come in here and sit next to each other on the couch. I love it when they lean into one another even though the couch is long, cutting off their own space.

"Listen," Pat says. "There's a whole world out there. How old are you?"

"Thirty-three, if you have to know."

"Keep going, man. You'll be full manager. What would you do if you were the manager right now? If I said, Theo, you are now the manager of Hoff Bagels. I'm talking profit sharing. The whole business. What would you do?"

I look at Pat slyly. "I'd change the world," I tell him, putting down my beer. "If I was manager there'd be no more war."

Pat looks at me for a second like he's going to laugh, but then he gets the joke and a queer expression passes over his face. It's like somebody's taken the air out of him. He sips on the bottom of his whiskey shot and then chases it with his beer. I give him a blank stare. "Yeah, well," he says, and I feel guilty already. "No need to worry about that. Have another one, all right?"

"All right," I say.

I send Bell a note that I won't be able to see her anymore, then sign off the kiosk and go to help Valerie behind the counter. I don't know why I do it. Because nothing in my life has ever worked out quite the way I planned. Because I'm selfish. I do it because I'm lonely and when I don't see her it's worse and because after three years in San Francisco I don't know anybody. Because I don't want to be seen. I don't know anybody and I don't want anybody to know. Because she was so human the last time I saw her. Just a real person, not sure what her next move is. And I don't have room for that. I can't take care of her. No, no, no. And for reasons I'm unsure of. My small apartment. This city and all of the cities. No. And the jungles with their animals. People with their problems. The windows. I woke last night and grabbed at the end of my mattress. I wanted to tear all of the stuffing out of it. The windows. No. It's hard enough.

Valerie doesn't want to talk to me. One time Valerie asked me to walk her to the campsite. She said she was afraid to go alone. All of the homeless were there, below the highway, at the base of Bernal Heights. Shopping carts were everywhere and they had strung tarp among them. A large fire was burning from a steel drum and we saw the men and women huddled around it from across Cesar Chavez. I asked Valerie why she wanted to go there though I knew it was to see Philc. But I didn't understand that she had to go down beneath the highway and the thick traffic of Army Street, a six-lane-deep river to be crossed. It looked like hell to me, that place she was going, all the people and stray dogs. Valerie looked at me like she didn't know what I meant. "I'm not going there," I told her. Valerie crossed her arms. "You don't have to go there," I said. She thought about it but then she stepped into the street, wading through the traffic, and I watched for a minute and then followed. We climbed out the other side and nobody seemed to care who we were. We found Philc's tent near the back, where everybody threw away their trash. Paper and soiled, torn clothing were everywhere, piles strung against the steel mesh fence before the brick-yard. He was standing, throwing a knife into the dirt. There were a couple of men sitting nearby sipping on the last of a glass bottle and wiping their beards. One of the men had a bag of peeled carrots on his lap.

"Is that your bodyguard?" Philc sneered. Valerie left me and went over to him. "I've been doing speed. Watch this." He pushed Valerie over to a big tree. She seemed to know what to do. She leaned back against it with her arms straight at her sides and closed her eyes. She looked happy. "Are you guys watching?" he asked the two men. One of them nodded and the other grabbed a carrot stub from his bag. Philc picked up his knife, a truck rumbled over the steel girders sending a shiver through the small plot. Philc threw the knife, striking the tree right next to Valerie's head. But it didn't stick. It fell to the ground and landed bent at her feet.

"That's dangerous," I said.

"Fuck," Philc said, gathering his knife. Valerie had opened her eyes.

"Let's go," I told her.

"She's not going anywhere," Philc said, looking down at his knife, running his fingers along the blade like he was going to clean it.

"You go," Valerie said. "I'll be OK."

"She's safe with me." Philc's dirty face was full of challenge. "There's room for her in my tent." He emptied a bottle of water onto a rag. There didn't seem to be anything for me to do but go. I wasn't wanted and it was immediately obvious that Valerie wasn't going to leave unless I carried her out, and I wasn't going to do that. I didn't want to watch Philc throw knives at her head. I worked my way down the path and lowered myself back into the street.

It's game night. The tables are filled with people playing board games. Twenty people, maybe. This group comes here once a week. I don't know who they are. They show up here. They order some coffee. We stay open later than usual. They set up Monopoly, checkers, Parcheesi. Push the pieces. They play for hours.

"This is our strangest night," I say to Valerie. But she's still upset so she doesn't even answer. "Valerie, look at them," I say over her shoulder. She's wearing a Naked Raygun shirt. LAST TOUR EVER. She's cutting a bagel for a customer. She ignores me. "I don't even know what I want. If somebody asked me what I wanted I couldn't even begin to answer them."

"But nobody's asking, are they?"

"No," I say. She's facing me with the knife. Somebody shouts, "Yahtzee!" Valerie's lips, at the corners, point down. "Nobody is."

I clean up my apartment. It doesn't take long, it's such a small place. I knock on my neighbor's door and ask if I can borrow his broom and I sweep my floors. I fill a bucket with soap and water and wash the walls. I leave my hands in the dark, soapy water for a minute. I stand by the window and watch the action on the street below, the hookers and the police cruisers. If I was in Chicago now we'd watch television. We'd avoid the obvious questions. We'd make excuses for nothing until we were done and we could finally sleep. Then the phone starts ringing.

I buy Valerie a five-dollar bar of soap that smells like cucumber. I take out the trash. Lunchtime, Philc is standing across Valencia Street. He has scratches on his cheek and a new tattoo under his eye. I pass him on my way to pick up pizza slices for Valerie and myself. We look at each other but I just keep walking. It's three in the afternoon and the shop is empty except for the girl with the tattooed face who's on the nod at the last table in the back. I remember when that girl started coming around the neighborhood, with her Barbie doll lunchbox, looking to get high. People would say she was pretty, except for the tattoos. It's like she only had that one thing wrong with her. But that was enough. The blue ink obscures her face entirely. It runs from her ears and eyes and curls under her chin like a beard. She gets in cars and turns tricks down by Folsom Street.

Valerie has finished her slice and is throwing away the paper plate. She pours herself a soda and dumps three ounces of peach syrup into it. She wipes her mouth with her forearm and then puckers her lips.

The light is blinking on the machine and all of my windows are open. The workers from the factory are huddled around the white lunch truck.

You fucking punk bitch. You think you can send me an email saying you don't want to see me anymore and that's it? I don't know what kind of game you are playing. Be as close to a man as you can be and pick up the motherfucking phone or do something that makes me less inclined to rip your fucking thinning hair out by the pale roots. I really don't have time for your shit. You belong on your back with me suffocating you. Why do you think there is room for you? Don't you think I have my own problems? I will ambush you somewhere. I will leave permanent marks. I warn you, don't fuck with me. You can't run away. I will be there tomorrow and if you are not available your whole neighborhood will know what a sissy punk bitch who likes to be raped you are. Don't underestimate my cruelty.

At work I stand near the counter. "C'mon," Valerie says. I take a breath before wrapping the last bagel of the morning in paper and handing it to the customer who walks out the door with it. Outside they're routing traffic around Valencia and the cars, each pointing in a slightly different direction, seem to be trying to climb over one another but none of them are moving. The cars need to get through. There is no way around Valencia. It's starting to rain. People run past the windows with papers over their hats. Philc and Valerie are in the back with the recycling and the trash, having a cigarette under the porch hang. I open the newspaper; there's been an invasion. I look up and Philc is standing at the counter in front of me. "Hey," he says quietly. "We need to come to an understanding, bro." I fold the newspaper, slide it over by the cookies. "Valerie loves you. Do you know that, man? You're family. You are. I think we can make this work." He pulls a toothpick from his pocket and plays with it between his front teeth. "Maybe we can all get a place together. You know what I mean? The three of us. No more bad times." He speaks calmly and I wonder what kind of pills he's been taking and if they would do me any good and how long they would last. "Friends for life?" He stretches his hand across the counter. I take his hand because every small bit of peace is worth having.

I put the bagels away and wrap the day-old pastries. Valerie comes back to help me. The rain is beating down on the sidewalk and Philc is sitting quietly in the back making origami from napkins.

That time you were tied up before. You looked so inno-cent. I wanted to draw blood. But I didn't. Do you know why? You like to think you're smart so you think other people can't understand you. You are so funny! Did you ever think I was reasonable? I mean, I can be a reasonable person but I don't like being played with. You cannot spend time with me and then send some pathetic excuse to disappear. Is that how you handle things? By running away? It doesn't work like that little boy. Answer your phone next time I call.

I tell Ambellina I'm sorry and ask if I can take her to see *Casablanca* at the Paramount in Oakland. It's been raining every day and I head to the East Bay. The Paramount is an Art Deco theater from the Depression that plays classic movies. The theater opens early for cocktails and the Wurlitzer. I'm there first, above the 19th Street BART station and after fifteen minutes I start to worry that she isn't going to show up and then she is standing in front of me. I try to take her hand but she won't let me. "What do you think you were trying to pull?" she asks. We're moving with the crowd of people down the street.

"I..."

"You what? Do you belong to me or not?" Men are watching her. She's wearing thigh-high latex yellow boots, fishnets, a leather skirt. Her tight curls are cut close to her scalp and dyed fire-engine red. She seems to be looking around, smiling at all of them at once. She also seems to be focused on only me.

"Yes," I say quietly.

"What?"

"Yes. I belong to you, Mistress." The guy walking next to me snickers.

We move through the large doors of the old theater, the heavily carpeted floors, velvet curtains, columns and statues reaching to a roof that ends in a midnight sky. The theater was built to hold thousands. Ambellina sends me for Coke and popcorn and when I come back the seats around us are filled up and the man in the coat and tails at the Wurlitzer is being lowered beneath the stage.

Bogart's face fills the screen and out of the corner of my eye I see that Ambellina is rummaging through her purse. I grew up with Humphrey Bogart. We had a television and my father loved the old Bogart films and would make me watch them whenever they were on. *Casablanca, The Maltese Falcon, Key Largo.* "You're not big enough to take me down, see." In his better moods my father would quote Bogart. "Sure, on the one hand maybe I love you and maybe you love me. But you'll have something on me you can use whenever you want. And since I'll have something on you who's to say you're not going to knock me over like you did the rest of them?" My father was a big man with a loud laugh, four inches taller than I am now. He was a violent man who wouldn't stand for being looked at crossways by women or children. He pushed my kindergarten teacher down a small flight of stairs. He was like a hurricane continually destroying our small house. He terrorized everyone within twenty feet. He was lazy and his laziness made him a criminal.

Bogart seems friendly to me among the roulette wheels and the card tables. His confidence. His big sad eyes. The white linen suits moving casually across the screen while the world is at war all around them. Rick's, a little Free French outpost on the sand. He does what he has to. He betrays poor Peter Lorrie to the Nazis. But the world won't let him alone. The world is bigger than the castle he has built for himself. This is the lesson of *Casablanca.*

Ambellina forces the gag into my mouth and I catch my breath. I let out a tiny moan while the big, round puck forces open my jaw and cheeks, sending a throbbing up the sides of my face.

"Shhh."

The theater is so quiet except for the actors and Ambellina slowly rubbing her thumb and index finger together. There's a hole in the puck to breathe through and I feel her pulling the straps around the back of my neck and fastening it tight to hold the gag in. I grip on to the seats. The strap catches and pulls my hair. I want to move out of this. To squirm. To wriggle down to the floor. I jerk my head one way, and then back. One quick breath. I push back in my seat, my feet pressing the floor. I try to hold the middle and when I can't I lean cautiously into Ambellina's shoulder, and she lets me stay there. Before the plane flies away I've grown used to the pressure against the roof of my mouth. When the lights come on I'm resting; I can hardly feel my hair caught in the buckle.

Tears

THE FOG HAS CLEARED UP TODAY, burning back over the park and bridges to the ocean. The past three days have been grey and yesterday the mail didn't come. This morning the fog was wrapped around the radio towers on top of Twin Peaks, flattened all the way down Eureka Valley, so from my windows even the 17 REASONS sign on Mission Street was obscured. I left my blinds open and stayed in bed with a book until almost noon. I didn't even try to do anything this morning with the fog like that, not even the dishes in the sink. I waited until the sun came out.

It takes almost an hour for me to get from my house in San Francisco to Mountain View, a suburban silicon town south of the city. I park my small car on a tree-lined street, away from the center. It's Saturday afternoon, sunny and hot and distinctly quiet on this road. She'd said her name was Jezebel but it's impossible to know for sure. Nobody uses their real name anymore. I lean against the mailbox, stare at the porcelain cat in the corner on the porch.

"You're late," Jezebel says to me. She looks just like her picture, which I had deliberately not looked at too closely. A round face and large hips. Flaming red hair. Spanish perhaps, or Italian. "Are you going to come in or not?"

"Sorry."

I follow her through the vestibule into her living room where we both sit down on a coffee brown two-piece couch. The room is well-organized, nice dishes in a glass breakfront, plants near the windows. There's a bowl on the coffee table with nothing in it. The bowl is clean, like it was just dusted. "So this is my house."

"It's a nice house."

"It's boring."

"It's nicer than my place. I live in a studio."

"I got it in the divorce. Do you smoke?"

"No," I tell her. "I don't smoke."

She puts a cigarette in her mouth and waits so I lean forward and grab her lighter from the coffee table and light her cigarette for her. "I got the house in the divorce," she says again. "I'm tired of pretending to want things I don't want and waiting for people to tell me what they want, hoping that maybe our desires match.

I'm running out of time for that. We only have so much time, you know?"

She leans back on her couch. The shades are up and spears of light puncture the living room. "I agree with you totally," I say. "I've been in a closet my whole life."

She crosses her leg over her knee, the heel of her shoe pointing at me. "The last guy I dated was this great-looking Norwegian. He looked like Thor with long blond hair and I'm just hoping that he likes to be hurt. Of course he doesn't. Waste of time." I nod my head. "So why don't you tell me what you want," she says.

"Well it's like I said in my ad…"

"I want a real man, OK. So while we're playing, if we play, then I'm in control, fine. I mean, I like to hurt people, I just do. And you like to be hurt, which is why you're over here. I think people can be honest about their desires. But don't ask me to dress you in women's clothes. I'm not going to sissify you. If I wanted a woman I'd be a lesbian. Don't think I don't get offers. No strap-ons either. I'm not going to use a strap-on on you. I want somebody who is masculine, but who wants to be hurt."

"I want to be hurt," I say.

"Well, I hope so." She moves forward and stubs out her cigarette. Takes another one from the pack and lights it herself. She's wearing the same velour pants that she was wearing in her picture. Whenever I find myself in situations like this I start to second-guess myself, question what I'm doing here. She's sizing me up now. It's past too late.

"Why don't you take your shirt off," she says. "You can hang it by the entryway. You might as well take your shoes off while you're there."

I put my shoes near the door, hang my shirt on a hook next to a fur jacket. I take my socks off and stick them in my shoes and return to her in just my jeans.

"Come here," she says and I slide across the couch toward her. "No. Don't be stupid. On the floor. Kiss my shoes. Good. The heels. Suck on the heel. There. Just a little bit. Use your tongue. Now say thank you."

"Thank you."

"Thank you what?"

"Thank you Mistress."

"Maybe we should go to the bedroom."

I have a memory. I'm fourteen. My father has left me in the basement of our house in Chicago. He's handcuffed me to a pipe and I'm miserable. "Don't break that pipe," he's said before leaving. I can see the bushes outside from where I'm sitting with my arm over my head. There are bushes all around that house and a thick green lawn. The basement is heavy with dust. I'm waiting, afraid to do anything as simple as break the pipe. I've been living on the streets for a year. Anyway, it's all over. Eventually he returns, saddened, his cheeks sliding from his face. Mother has only just passed away. We blame each other for that. I blame the screams, the constant noise. He's slipping the key into the cuffs. "One day you'll understand," he says, the shackles falling from my wrist. "When you're older." I exit the basement back to the streets.

Jezebel ties me to the bed using basic laundry rope. She wraps the rope around my ankles, spreading my legs, pulling my feet toward the posts. It's a small bedroom with a bed, a dresser, and a wall full of mirrored tile. I can see myself. "Do you like to be tied up?" she asks.

"Yes," I say. "I really do."

"You have to tell me what you want. Don't expect me to know what you want. I'm not a mind reader you know." She's tying my arms above my head. I worry that the knots are not secure, and that I'm not helpless. I worry that it would be possible for me to escape. "Do you want a blindfold?"

"Whatever you want," I say.

"What did I tell you? You have to communicate." She looks at me spread naked on her bed and shakes her head. Then she looks at the bedroom door, which is still open. She bites her lip like she's considering leaving.

"Please," I say quietly, turning my cheek into the bed. It's just a whisper. "Do whatever you want to me. I don't want to know."

"But you have to tell me. You don't even know me. I need to know what you're into. What are your limits?

What if I peed on you? What if I left you here and came back tomorrow? Only an idiot would say something like that."

"Please," I say. "Don't leave."

She takes her clothes off, stripping down to red underwear and a red bra. Her skin is pale orange and rolls of fat hang around her waist, contrasting her legs, which are thin and long like a bird's. "Lift your head up." She wraps the blindfold around my eyes but I can still see a vein of light beneath it. "I was honest in my advertisement. You obviously were not. I said very specifically I wanted someone who could communicate. Someone who knew what they wanted. You clearly do not know what you want." I feel her nails pinching my nipples. Hard. And then harder.

"Ow. Ow. Ow! Ow! Owowow! Please. Please, it hurts. It hurts."

"Please what?"

"Please Mistress."

"So that's too much for you?" I don't answer her. I keep my mouth closed. Then she slaps me. "Is it? Is it or isn't it? How impossible for you? Do you know how to talk?"

"I don't know, Mistress. I don't know."

"Well you're going to have to know." I feel the weight of her shin against my throat, her hand on my chest, the sheet moving beneath me, and then her body on my face. She's taken her underwear off and I'm surrounded by the smell of her. I can't breathe except when she lifts off of me. "Get your tongue in there." I stick my tongue out gingerly and feel a pain shoot up my stomach from between my legs and she is bouncing on top of my head. "You're going to have to do a lot better than that. Make yourself good for something before I kick you out of here. Minus your clothes. Come on!" She punches me in the stomach and pushes against me, grinding her whole body into my face, rolling her body over me in waves, the weight of her body, the smell of her ass and her vagina, her large buttocks along my cheeks, the extra skin there, and the soft patches.

It's cold, and I can breathe again. She's tied my balls and penis with rope. "I'm going to fuck you," she says. My face is sticky with her. My face is covered in her smell.

"No," I say, trying to affect a measure of calm. "It's not safe. We have to have safe sex." She forces her underwear into my mouth and a first layer of panic washes across me. She pinches my nose for a second and fabric brushes the back of my throat and I cough. I feel her putting the condom on me. I try to focus on staying hard. I have no interest in sex. I think of the pictures of the women I look at on the Internet, muscular women fighting on rubber mats, sitting on each other's faces, matchbook holds. Usually the women are still wearing leotards. I think of one video clip, my favorite, where the wrestler straddles the other woman, pulls her legs up toward her shoulders, then lands an open-hand slap between the other girl's thighs. I think of being raped by a group of transexuals with large penises and enormous breasts, beaten and overpowered and held down against my will in a hotel room above a bar on Polk Street and walking home with a bloody lip and a black eye afraid to tell anyone what I've done. Or just one thin Asian woman with a strap-on putting lipstick on my mouth, taking me from behind gently, whispering in my hair, her arm around my chest and another between my legs, holding me like her submissive female lover. I think of these things to stay hard for Jezebel while she rides on top of me, desperately riding over me and then stopping.

"What are you doing?" she says. She climbs off of me. Her hand whips across my face and I whimper into the underwear. She's straddling my chest. "What are you doing here? Are you dysfunctional? If you can't get it on with me you can't get it on with anybody. That's why you have to go online to meet women, try to meet women on the personal ads."

"You're killing her," my father says. He's standing in my room. My arms are over my head, everything is broken, even pieces of the wall are lying on the floor. His face is burning and covered in perspiration, sweat seeping into the violent lines along his forehead. "You're killing your mother the way you act." He's stopped screaming now, and I'm shivering all over, his voice still vibrating through my body. He's wearing his uniform, the long stick dangling from his belt, badge pinned against his jacket. My mother is paralyzed on the couch, still awake but unable to say anything. The woman who will soon be my stepmother inhabits the kitchen, a floating grey ghost.

"What kind of person has to do what you do?" she says, hitting me again, and then again. Then grabbing my hair. "Tell me. Tell me! Say something. This is worthless, this thing lying here. This is worthless. You will never make anybody happy with this and you'll never be happy yourself. You will be lonely till the day you die." I feel the moisture gathering beneath the blindfold. The tears soaking the cloth. The room is so hot. "I'm supposed to feel sorry for you now? You're pathetic. Why did you come here?" I open my mouth but only make small, animal sounds, stuck with long strands of spit. The tears come long and fast now, and the moans and cries. It seems endless. I feel like I could cry forever, choking. I feel the weight of her on my chest, the comfort of the ropes keeping my limbs apart. I feel her climbing from me. Her feet on the floor, her hands stroking my stomach and the air rushing into my mouth and nose. "It's OK," she says. "It's OK."

It's just like she said in her ad. Dacryphilia, arousal from tears. *I want to make you cry*. I wanted to meet her for this reason. *Your tears are precious to me.* It feels so good to cry. Everything bad runs out of me in the tears that run down my cheeks, over my ears, soaking the bed beneath me. I feel the rope going slack on my arms and then my legs.

"That's better now."

I pull my legs into my chest, my elbows to my knees.

"Come on. It's over." I tighten into a ball. "Come on. Oh fuck." I hear her leaving, walking from the room. I stay in my own darkness, my body turning over, the sheets building up along my edges. It's a while before she comes back and I've gotten cold. "Get out."

I unstretch. Stand in front of the bed, stuck between the bed and the wall trying not to touch the glass, pulling my jeans on. "I'm sorry," I say.

"I was honest in my ad. I can't stand liars."

"I'm sorry."

"You're sorry." She looks away from me, exhaling. She's dressed in a sweater and sweatpants and her hands are on her hips. "You're selfish is what you are." I follow her to the front where she watches me put on my shoes and then my shirt. "You should just say: sissy boy, into infantilism, shy. Looking for mommy."

"But I wanted to cry," I say.

"I'm a person too, you know. I'm not a bad person. I don't deserve to be taken advantage of and have my time wasted. What did I ever do to you?"

The sun is still burning horrifically across the South Bay hills and the looming billboards. Coming back into San Francisco I pass the casino in Colma surrounded by graveyards, construction and metal mess around the airport, the greasy water of the Bayshore, and the giant sign just before the city: SOUTH SAN FRANCISCO, THE INDUS-TRIAL CITY, standing in large steel beams against a dull green hillside. And the ribbon of the highways and all of the people on them, the sharp point of the Transamerica Pyramid puncturing the sky. Couples in cars. Everybody going somewhere.

Three Men and a Woman

EDEN AND I ARE IN AN ART GALLERY that doubles as a dance club. A DJ stands on a sheet of plywood over milk crates playing house music with a heavy bass line. It's still afternoon, but already there are a few office workers here loosening their ties, putting their earrings back in.

With us is David. He and Eden have known each other fifteen years, since high school. He has flushed cheeks, feminine features, wears black jeans and a leather jacket. He helps Eden clean, shop, run chores, carries her things. Eden refers to David as her pockets. David refers to Eden as his girlfriend. Girlfriend, he feels, comes closest to summing up their relationship.

I tell him I think he should use a paragraph. That a word isn't going to explain it. But what is probably bothering me more is that *girlfriend* is the term I've been using. She told me she doesn't like it but I use it anyway, perhaps for the same reason David does.

My paragraph would have to include that Eden is married. That there is a child at the house four days a week. That not only is she married but she also has David, meaning there are three men in her life minimum. That what we have is not nonmonogamy, it is polyamory. That I love her and that I think this could maybe work sometimes and then other times I see nothing but a bunch of potholes, a couple of landmines, and a trainwreck.

The after-work crowd is trickling in. Button-ups have been replaced with undershirts. I talk with David and watch Eden dance. She kicks her legs, spins. She looks like a fighter in a ring, her dark hair pulled back, swinging her fists halfway, elbows bent. She's a very good dancer but she looks best when she curves her back, as if she was dancing to something gothic, preparing to bite someone on the neck. Other times, she tilts at hard angles, keeping her body protected.

"Fish swim," David says. "Birds fly, Eden dances."

"I have to dance with her," I say. "Before she dances with someone else."

"It's not a zero-sum game," he says.

I don't even know what he means. He's trying to help me. I'm trying to understand him. Already there are three men dancing near her, all of them turned to show their availability.

The day I met Eden's husband, I was crossing the bridge
and called to say I would be there shortly. The bay was
filled with tankers nosing into port and sailboats like
pieces of paper. I was just rolling onto the span over
Treasure Island, could already see the landfill, the
abandoned military facilities. Eden said, "OK, come
over."

"You don't want to wait on the corner?" I asked.
What's wrong with corners, I thought. Corners are nice.

"You have to meet him eventually," she replied.

They live back from the street in a two-bedroom
mud-colored bungalow. I was standing in the doorway
when he stepped out of the kitchen. The meeting was
awkward but not awful. "Oh," he said as we shook hands.
He was better looking than I expected and three inches
taller than I. He wore light jeans and a striped shirt. I
was wearing a necklace, leather pants, and a sleeveless
top. We both looked our roles: the suburban father and
the other man.

I could hear Eden speaking with their son in the
other room. Her husband and I made some small talk
about his job, and then Eden and I were gone. I try not
to question Eden's marriage or her situation with David.
It's not my place to second-guess other people's desires.
One evening I confessed that I didn't understand her
relationship with her husband.

She laughed. "You don't even understand *our* relationship."

Eden and I make each other CDs, see movies together, go shopping. We sit late into the night telling stories about our families. Eden's father kicked her out when she was fifteen. I left home when I was thirteen and never went back. The truth is this is the healthiest relationship I've ever had. When I tell her I am worried that between David, her husband, and her job she won't have enough time for me, she says, "Tell me what you need to make this work."

I see Eden about four days a week, and on days when I don't see her we talk on the phone. She's negotiating with her husband for a night each week to spend at my apartment. She'd like to see a situation where I come over for big family events, like Thanksgiving and New Year's. But none of us are ready for that.

She and I have moved so quickly and had so many opportunities to fail. Eden says that my lack of relationship experience is usually a red flag for her. I say being married is usually a red flag for me. Her husband is upset because having multiple sexual partners is one thing and falling in love is something else. She says this is the first time she's fallen in love since meeting her husband nine years ago.

The music is louder, the room hotter, the crowd thickening in the club, all of us with hearts stamped on the inside of our wrists.

"I almost didn't show up one day," Eden says, resting her wrists on my shoulders. "I panicked."

"If you hadn't showed up I would have been so dis-appointed," I say.

"I would have called," she says.

"That wouldn't have helped."

David sits while we dance. I wonder if he is not some mirror for me; if he wasn't real I would create him. I like David. I have a magazine in my bag and I want to offer it to him, but it's too dark to read. I wonder how much of his life he spends watching Eden dance, her jacket next to him, her cigarettes in his pocket. I ask myself if I could do what he's doing. If I could sit for hours and watch Eden dance with other people. The first answer that comes to mind is no. No, it's a waste of life. But the second answer is yes. Yes, if she wasn't going home to her husband. If she was going home with me. If we were going to sleep together, if I was going to lie next to her in my bed, beneath her. If she was going home with me I could wait all night. But she isn't.

Not long ago Eden came over to my apartment. She was late and I looked from my window and saw a black car pause and then continue down the street. I thought it was her car and I went downstairs. I thought maybe she couldn't find parking and would come back around and I would get in and we would drive together. But the car never came back and I began to break. It was a week-end and the sun was out. It was unbearably hot and bright enough to see all the broken glass, dirt, and old paint stains on the curb. By the time an hour had passed my face was burning.

And then she arrived. Wearing a patterned summer skirt and a spaghetti-strap top, carrying a heavy bag. I laughed when I took the bag from her. "I thought I saw your car," I kept saying. But she'd just been stuck in a traffic jam on the bridge. She doesn't have a cell phone. She kept stroking my head saying, "You poor baby." I was inches away from crying. I pushed my face into her collar, gripped her tightly.

Inside the club we sit apart from David. He doesn't know where we are but we're only ten feet away. Eden and I are exhausted from dancing. Our shirts are soaked. The club is full and people climb around us, hiding their jackets below our bench and their sweaters on the ledge above. We're cushioned and surrounded by their clothing.

One time she said to me, "I haven't placed any limits on you. You place limits on yourself." And to help I've been reading a book about polyamory. The book recommends you own your decisions. No one can make you do anything. The important thing is not to get in a cycle of blame, the book says, but rather to inform your partner of your feelings. Most relationships are doomed anyway; it's their nature.

I squeeze Eden's arms as she turns, throwing her legs over mine. When I first met her I was shocked by her raw physical beauty. I didn't think the fact that she was in an open marriage would affect me one way or the other. I wasn't thinking long term. I had no idea of Eden's capacity for affection. Some think that love is a finite resource, like food. That love given to one person is love taken from someone else. Others believe that the more you love the more love you're capable of. It's what enables families to have more than one child.

To make this work I have to be clear about what my needs are. I'm going to be strong, I think. Because if I'm not strong I'm going to crack and if I crack I'm going to sink and there's not going to be any returning to the surface.

Outside it's gotten cold. I peel my shirt off and replace it with three layers I brought for the bike ride home. Recently a woman I've always liked who lives in New York confessed she'd like to tie me up next time I was in town. I asked Eden if it was OK and she told me she was jealous. It was my first time suggesting another woman.

"I know it's hypocritical," Eden said. After five days she decided it was fine, that it was probably even good for us. She said people who claim not to be jealous are fooling themselves, it's just what you do with it.

I walk David and Eden to her car. They're going back across the bay, where the giant grocery stores are. I'm staying here in the city, where it's crowded. I've always lived in cities and I've wondered if this city is even big enough, if there are enough people. I like crowds, diversity, opportunity.

I kiss Eden at the overlit parking garage. The theater-goers insert bills and punch buttons on the bright yellow machines. David lingers near the corner, one elbow on a newspaper box.

I'm seeing her tomorrow, in the evening. Tomorrow is Thursday and David will be there. And then I won't see her until Tuesday. Eden will be home soon and I'll sleep alone tonight. I think about the long weekend looming as I bicycle past the hot neon signs South of Market, too dark to see the potholes now.

I'll Love You Back

OUTSIDE IT'S RAINING. The clouds seem to want to break and I think maybe they will, in an hour or two. And when they do I'll have to close the curtains and the shades because the sun hits my windows and covers me while I'm trying to write.

I'm working on a story about a group home I lived in for almost two years when I was an adolescent. I lived in five different homes in Chicago between the ages of fourteen and eighteen and spent a year sleeping on a rooftop before that. I went to four different high schools. Almost everything I've written has been influenced by things that happened to me during those years. I've never been very good at writing fiction.

My girlfriend, Eden, wants me to wear a plug while I'm working. She likes to be in control. It's a large sili-cone purple plug. I cover it with Liquid Silk before sliding it in. It hurts going in and then it doesn't. The shaft is much thinner than the head. I have to breathe for a moment, feel her inside me taking up space. I sit on a towel in a padded black chair. I'm afraid to move. This is one of the last places of taboo in our relationship. When we first got together I told her I wasn't comfortable being dominated by her when she wasn't around. I didn't think I'd be able to get work done wearing nipple clamps or not being allowed to masturbate or having a plug up my ass, which is what I have now. But in a way it doesn't matter. When Eden comes over, when she spends the night, it usually takes a day to get over it anyway. She covers me with bites, bruises, cuts. Her name is carved in my back. She's with me all the time, or I'm longing for her. She leaves a velvet bag of rope next to my bed. Sometimes I think it's unfair. She's with me when she isn't.

I've been having a hard time working anyway. It would be impossible to say, if I don't get any work done, if it is just my continuing writer's block or the object in my ass. Victor Hugo once said, when asked if it was hard to write *The Hunchback of Notre-Dame*, "My dear, it's either easy or it is impossible."

The story I'm trying to write is a true story but I mean to write it as fiction. I don't want to defend the truth of my recollections. I had just turned seventeen and was sleeping beneath a thin blanket on the living room floor of the group home. I was naked. The carpet was green and scratchy. Upstairs the other boys were asleep in the bedrooms. This particular group home looked just like a normal two-story house in a quiet middle-class neighborhood in Chicago. It was not a violent place. I had been in other homes significantly worse. Locked facilities with red lines painted along the floors and shit smeared across the walls. Places built a hundred years ago, where the doors locked from the outside and you left your shoes in the hallways at night. Square concrete buildings with slit windows in state compounds hidden by high fences and miles of untended lawn, out of sight and mind from the taxpaying public. Shelters with thirty children to a room and nobody with anything left to lose. I did not have a happy childhood.

I'd had sex once already. Not counting the times I was molested. I was fifteen and I was with Tom and Maureen who lived across from the home in an apartment with Maureen's parents. They were both in their twenties. Tom worked the construction truck owned by Maureen's father and sometimes I worked with him. It was just a white truck with a red stripe along the side and we drove around the western edges of Chicago looking for houses that needed tuck-pointing. Tom was eight years older than me and grew up in many of the same homes I had been in. He was well over six feet tall with the largest arms I'd ever seen. We sat in the back of the truck with the hawks and slicks and bags full of sand. If it was raining we'd cover ourselves in tarps; if it was sunny we'd take our shirts off and feel the wind whip across our sun-drenched backs. Maureen's father gave me twenty-five dollars for twelve-hour days and I mixed barrows full of cement and loaded pallets with mortar while Tom climbed the ladders, sixty-pound rolls of tar balanced on his shoulders, leaning into the rails.

After work we bought beer and drugs and went back to Maureen and Tom's two rooms. Maureen's room was covered in pictures of Elvis but we never listened to him. We listened to the Ramones and the Defoliants. We were smoking pot laced with PCP and taking horse-pill-sized downers. Maureen's friend Kat was there. Kat was nineteen and kind. She worked the front desk at a motorcycle dealership on Broadway. She always wore cutoff jeans and a bikini top. She said she liked virgins. She took me into the back room, stripped me naked, and climbed on top of me. She was thin from too much speed but still young enough to look healthy. I was too stoned to move but I was glad to not be a virgin anymore. I couldn't feel her sliding up and down my penis but I watched as I disappeared inside her pubic hair then reappeared again. The lights were off but I could see everything. It was like being covered in glitter. I hadn't asked what was in the pills they gave me. I took anything that passed under my nose.

"C'mon," she said. I didn't know what she meant. She got off me and showed me how to mount her, guiding me in. She showed me how to fuck her from behind. She got my dick into her ass. I saw Tom and Maureen watching from the bottom of the doorway. They looked happy.

"I can't make you come," Kat said, pushing against me, her back fluorescent with sweat. She reached back and grabbed my side. Later she went to the schoolyard and asked my friends if they had heard about what happened between us. Some said they had. "It's all true," she told them.

The night I slept naked in the living room things were looking up. I had quit drugs. I didn't hang out with Tom, Maureen, and Kat anymore. I was taking double classes during summer session in the normal high school and it looked like I would graduate on time after all, even though I missed my first two years of study. I had stolen my own air conditioner and sold it for a half gram of coke six months before, which is why I was in the living room; it was very hot that night.

It was probably around midnight when I woke up next to Sheila. She was the group home manager. She spent three nights a week in the home. She had crawled under my blanket and was looking at me. She had enormous hazel eyes.

"Hi," I said, or maybe I didn't say anything. It's hard to know. I'm trying to remember if this is a happy story or a sad story. If it's a sad story I would mention that Tom, my good friend who hooked me up with my first consensual sexual encounter, died of a heroin overdose fifteen years later a few days before Christmas. He bucked on his dealer's floor, foaming at the mouth, eyes wide and white, choking on an unreleased scream, powerful fingers digging into the ground, wood chips catching beneath his nails, while his dealer sat above him searching the Internet for a cure. It's easy to make fun but a lot of people I knew then didn't make it.

Sheila asked if she could have a hug and I said yes, of course, because I was seventeen and she was twenty-five and I was in love with her the way I was always in love with beautiful women in positions of power over me. More so because she gave me books to read like *Zen and the Art of Motorcycle Maintenance* and *Diet for a Small Planet*, and read me poetry I didn't understand. She was the only adult who had shown sustained interest in my life. I didn't know what she needed the hug for or what to do. Sheila was tall and thin with large breasts, curly hair and a long nose. She would sunbathe in a bikini in the backyard, tiny brown hairs poking out along her thighs. I would watch her while the other kids shot baskets against the garage.

My memories are complicated by the plug up my ass and the knowledge that I will be seeing Eden later and it is hard to get turned on thinking about anybody else. I wonder if I loved Sheila then the way I love Eden now. Earlier in the week I met Eden at the house where she works. It was her birthday and I brought her chocolates and a sweater. I sat at her feet while she changed from her work clothes—fishnets, high heels, corset—into blue jeans and a white shirt and tie. She was changing from girl to boy. Her clients had given her boots and bouquets and a rattan cane. "I'm going to use this on you," she said, showing me the cane as we drove into the hills overlooking the bay. "You can only use these on one person. There's no way to clean the blood off."

I put my arm around Sheila and tried not to touch her with my erection. I was leaking pre-come. She was wearing a denim skirt. Her hair smelled like syrup. She pushed toward me, pressing her breasts against my chest. She was smiling. I think we lay like that for half an hour but I could have stayed for a week. In retrospect she was clearly waiting for me to do something, but that seemed impossible to me. I was an ugly child, fucked once from kindness. I had fantasized about Sheila, masturbated imagining her tying me up and suffocating me by sitting on my face. Or coming home from school one day and finding Sheila sitting on the chair in the smoking room with her dress pulled up and her knees exposed and patting her lap and me lying across her and her pulling my pants down to my ankles and spanking me. I imagined her dressing me in women's panties, putting me on a leash with a collar, and humiliating me in front of the other staff members. But those were just fantasies and at seventeen I hoped they would go away once I had a regular girlfriend. They never did. Instead they developed into a fetish for being burned and cut and spit on,

murder fantasies, trauma games, edge play, sensory dep-
rivation, a reckless desire to be harmed. I'm lucky that
I've ended up with Eden, who takes pleasure in hurting
me but never does so out of anger and tells me all the
time how special I am and how good and how much she
loves me and appreciates it when I raise my ass higher
for another swat from her cane until my thighs and ass
are covered with bleeding welts and I am crying like a
child and she is stroking my cheek saying, "Come back
to me little boy." But at seventeen that was all in a bottle,
buried deep somewhere. I was trying to make do. It was
enough that I was going to school. I would become a
poster child for the potential of troubled children to
make a turnaround. This group home was the best place
I'd lived in. Nobody got strapped to a bed or locked in
a time-out room. We weren't fed Kool-Aid dosed with
Thorazine or strip-searched and prodded by thick-
armed security guards with other intentions. I had
already survived those places; I was going to make it
even though I didn't have a support network except for
a handful of friends, all of them more messed up than
me. The staff at the group home changed every few
months. There was no consistency. Sheila would be gone
soon. She was already engaged to a man who managed
a local rock-and-roll band. I didn't like him. He came
over and watched baseball games. He sat on the couch
and never said a word. I thought he didn't pay her
enough attention and I told her so.

The night was so hot and uncomfortable. I waited for what Sheila would do. I could smell her lips. The curtains were lit by orange streetlights. There was no sound from outside. She gave me a piece of paper with her address and phone number. Pushed it against my rib cage. Told me to come over after school. She had everything to lose, her future husband, her job, her license. She could go to jail. But I didn't think about any of that. She was the group home mom. The closest thing I had to a parent. I stayed awake with my hard-on, rubbing against the carpet, facedown with my hands between my legs, cheek pressed into the floor. It was four in the morning when I ventured into her bedroom.

"You couldn't sleep either?" she asked.

I asked her for a cigarette and we smoked in her bed. I had a history test in the morning. She sat up against the pillows. And then I leaned in close and we started to kiss. My hand went immediately to her breast. I still remember what that felt like, heavy but soft and hidden beneath the thin cotton of a grey shirt. I felt her nipple through the fabric and the bumps around it. She held my arm. She wasn't pulling me closer or pushing me away. Her skirt sat on top of the dresser. She was sitting with her legs crossed partially covered by a blanket. I touched the inside of her thigh. She was wearing white underwear with pink dots. I almost touched the elastic with my pinky finger. I could see her dark mound of hair inside the cotton. Her mouth tasted like sour granola and eventually she pulled back and I kissed her one more time. "Tomorrow," she said, though it was already tomorrow.

There were thirty of us in the room taking the test. It was against school rules to wear shorts. Two teachers sat in the front talking. They weren't worried about anybody cheating. After school I passed the football players practicing in jerseys and pads in front of the building. They lay on their backs in the grass kicking their legs. They looked like blue turtles.

I took the bus across the city. There were no clouds that summer. Sheila lived near the lake in a three-flat. It was a long apartment with dark hardwood floors and I could just see downtown from one of her windows. She had two roommates but they weren't home. There were books everywhere and album covers tacked to the walls. "Let's not stay here," she said. We were in her dining room. There was a square table and a picture of half-naked people camping in the desert. I stood at the edge of the table. Her hair was tied in a long, curly ponytail. "Let's go for a walk."

At the park was a fair and women with strollers were carrying giant swaths of cotton candy. There was a Mexican band playing. People were eating buttered corn on a stick. The grass was worn away from being walked on. Sheila said, "I talked to my friend and it's really not a good idea." She said it like I would agree with her, as if it was obvious. We walked closely, slightly brushing each other's arms.

"OK," I said. It was the only thing I could say without betraying myself. I didn't know her friend or what she had told her. I didn't even ask her about the idea that wasn't good, though I would have liked to know. Not a good idea for who? I wanted to know exactly what I had missed. What had I done wrong? I wanted her so badly. I wanted her to adopt me. I could stay in her bed with her and her fiancé who ignored her. I didn't care. What I really wanted to say was that I loved her and I thought there was a way we could make it work, that there's a solution to every problem, when of course there isn't.

We watched the band for a while and Sheila bought a chopped mango, which we shared. I walked her back to her apartment. It was still very bright out. She suggested going to the lake then changed her mind.

"Maybe we should call it a day."

The story has no climax. Sheila quit the home soon after that and the next woman who came to run the home locked the door on me so I moved into a friend's basement where I stayed for nine months before starting college. Sheila called me on my eighteenth birthday and I met her at a cafe and she gave me a bicycle, which was a big present. I would use that bicycle until the frame rusted out and cracked and then I would leave it locked to a tree and never see it again.

When I took the bike from Sheila she said something encouraging, like "People care about you." I hadn't seen her in almost a year. The cafe we were at was called the

No Exit. Taxi drivers went there to play chess. I asked her about her boyfriend and his band. It didn't matter. Whatever window had opened that night was well shut and locked. Legally I was an adult. Sheila went to graduate school then and married her fiancé who probably never did find out about her small affair with the group home kid. Maybe it didn't count. She sent me letters occasionally and then stopped. For a long time I thought about her. I drew pictures of her face in all my notebooks. I went to college for a couple of years, then left to strip in gay clubs and star in bisexual porn videos. The hands reaching from the darkness in the clubs made me feel cold and alone. People put dollar bills in my underwear and made promises they had no intention of keeping. I went back to drugs for a while and woke up in an Evanston hospital paralyzed for eight days following a hotshot and a grand mal seizure. But I turned out OK eventually too, it just took me a little while to get to the point where I could write a story with a plug in my ass while waiting for the phone.

My Friend Petey

"TRY TO UNDERSTAND," I say. "It's not like that."

I'm talking to my oldest friend, Petey. He lives in Atlanta now in the worst part of a city that was supposed to be the hope of the new South. He says after the hurricane the drug cartel moved in from New Orleans, making a bad situation worse. He says they've built around and over his neighborhood. Five people get shot every day. He wants to get back to Chicago, where we're from, where he has a child he left behind. He has to be in Chicago if he's going to file the paperwork and take it to court, if he's going to see his son.

"She's not going to leave her husband," I tell him. I'm talking about my girlfriend, not his. His girlfriend has filed a restraining order, changed her address, turned off her phone. My girlfriend is married. I live in San Francisco where this sort of thing is not so uncommon:

alternative relationships, polyamory, BDSM. He moved east, I moved west. I'm speaking to him from the 24th Street BART station. There are pimps and junkies with sliced towels wrapped around their arms, schizophrenics talking to themselves against the fence, a Chinese man with a Peavey amplifier preaching the love of Christ. But there's also cafes and a restaurant with seven-dollar hamburgers and four-dollar shakes and just a block away there's a place that's so popular it could take three weeks to get an eight o'clock table.

And I know where he's calling from, deep in the heart of a place he can't get out of. Where he lives he confronts violence every day. Nobody shores the mortar between the bricks and buildings are crumbling, the city center disintegrating, white flight, urban sprawl, sliding piles of stone and dust, highways stretching miles across the ghetto with no exit and no entrance ramp, the city spreading like syrup over hotcakes. He says it takes two hours and three buses to get to where he works for twenty-five cents above the minimum wage.

"Atlanta doesn't have very good public transportation," he tells me. His license has been revoked. He's not allowed to drive.

I remember twenty years ago when he was punched in the face in front of a hot dog stand and the blood exploded across the condiments and tiny paper buckets. I remember the boy that terrorized him and the man who molested him. He always had a knack for getting what he deserved and then some. I also know what he did to our friend's younger sister in a paneled apartment beneath the el tracks. Shrugged my shoulders when they called him a pedophile. Went with him to court when he testified and helped him hide when they put his face on the front of the newspaper next to the man he helped take off the street. The caption: *Drug dealer gets forty years for shooting homeless man with crossbow.*

We haven't spoken in a long time. I used to wake him up before school, rising an hour early so I could get to him on time. At night I'd do his homework while he shot baskets on the schoolyard. Nobody could figure out why I hung out with him but I liked him because he never had anything better to do.

"Have you met her husband?" he asks me. I tell him I have, twice.

"It wasn't as awkward as it sounds."

"He's going to confront you," he says. I can hear him thinking on the other side of the country, buried deep in that hole he stuck himself in when I stopped pulling him out—*Every situation comes to violence*—which makes perfect sense when it's all you know.

Our childhood mixed like paint. He knows who raped me, who pissed on my clothes when I spent my year sleeping in broom closets. He knew my father before my father was put away for pinging a child's fingertips with a hammer as the boy's chin rose above the windowsill to peer into my room. He knew my mother when all she could do was shake so violently she stuttered; before she didn't wake up, her insides pooling in her stomach, her body pale except for one enormous, silent bruise. And now I'm trying to explain that I'm in love with a married woman and it's as foreign to him as anything else. As the city I live in with all its colors where the ocean scales the cliff walls and the bay. As what I do for a living—telling stories, teaching classes. This is how different we've become. My current friends went to Ivy League schools. I don't even pay when I go to the theater. I get free books in the mail. He lives in a neighborhood redevelopment left behind, budgets his bus fare and eats quickly during lunch breaks off the clock. At work he wears a brown apron and a paper hat. And he has a son but he's not allowed to see him. He hasn't paid child support. There's a restraining order. He's not allowed to drive. It's been a long time since we shared everything, even our attackers.

He wants to know why I haven't called. I'm afraid to say I stopped caring about you because if I say so it might be true. This isn't about polyamory, it's about something else. I used to watch after him like a mother. I don't want to tell him how much it hurts sometimes and that I'm afraid no one will ever love me the most.

What I want to tell him is the other night my lover placed a gas mask over my face. The mask lowered like a spaceship and she ratcheted the straps tight. Naked and prone with my fingers laced behind my head, I saw her face, eyes creasing into a smile. She held the filter so I couldn't breathe and the latex hugged my cheeks. She pulled a blindfold across the sockets so I couldn't see anything anymore. And then she fucked me in the airless dark. For the first time I didn't think of the predators we shared when the state took us both, our small rooms and locked doors. I didn't think of Petey's dull features, his thick pale skin, his freckles and moles and dry red pubic hair. How he turned his large body against the wall when they came for me. What the cabinet looked like from my vantage point, bent across the desk in the staff offices while he pretended to sleep, the social worker's fingers spreading across the back of my neck.

We were raped. I eroticize my trauma while Petey claws his way to the rim of the American Dream. I panicked when my girlfriend pulled away. *I'm right here*, she said, touching my stomach until I calmed down. *I'll count so you know I'm close. One... Two...* I heard my labored breathing and her feet padding across the floor, glasses and books moving on my shelves. She was back on top of me before getting to ten, her thighs squeezing my ribs, a straight razor gently parting my skin. *One for every moment I've been away.* Nine small cuts across my chest, drips of blood on the bedsheet.

"We're in love," I say.

"If that's what you do in San Francisco," Petey replies.

Then he lets out that dumb laugh he's always had. The laugh of someone who doesn't understand anything.

The laugh of someone who is used to not understanding things and has decided to go along with it. It's exactly how he laughed when he made a shot on the basketball court: mouth open, tongue waggling over his teeth. We were waiting for people who weren't going to show. It's a laugh that reminds me of a day on the yard, bricks painted in epithets, a chill setting across the asphalt, before and during the time that everything went horribly wrong.

Just Always Be Good

THE FIRST THING EDEN DOES is take my clothes off
and tie me up. She uses a long black rope, starts with
my balls and my penis, continues to my ankles, then
from my wrists to my ankles, all of it a series of complicated knots. She wraps a collar around my neck and
ties the rope to the collar, so that almost any movement
pulls on my genitals. I'm going to New York tomorrow.
We're not going to see each other for twelve days.

I'm on the hardwood floor of my bedroom on my
back. I can put my feet down or my head, but not both.
She pushes me and I fall on my side. I've been tied up
many times but everything is different with Eden.

I once followed a woman into her apartment on the
Upper West Side. There were piles of stuffed animals as
high as our knees. The animals spilled onto the mattress,
which was uncovered. The walls were smeared in red

graffiti. There was a dog leashed to an open refrigerator. I realized only when it was too late that I had followed a crazy person home. She tied my arms over my head, blindfolded me, burned me all over my body with her cigarette. That's the kind of thing I used to do before Eden. I'd go home with anybody; I just wanted to be hurt. I have scars.

This is the opposite of that. This is a happy story.

Eden cradles my head in her lap, her bag nearby. Yesterday her mother had a biopsy. There was a chance Eden wasn't going to be able to come over today, depending how things went. Her mother may have cancer.

Eden has thick thighs, comfortable legs. I'm so far gone, so in love, I can barely think. I stare at her cheeks, her nose. I can see every pore, blood vessels below the surface of her skin, hairs that will turn grey one day.

Eden attaches a clip to my nipple. "Do you want another one?" she asks. "Yes please," I say. And that's how it goes, as my voice gets weaker and she lines my body with her clips, finally running a string of them down my penis. Every movement increases the pain.

"You're being so good," she says.

"I love you so much," I whisper back.

She strokes my face. I keep thinking to myself how nice she is, wondering why she is so nice to me. It makes me want to cry. We have the whole day. Her husband said she could spend the night; her son is away at camp. My roommate is home in the next room with his music turned up. That's the world around us. And then there is Eden and me and all the clips she's decorated me with, her initials carved across my back, the bruises on my belly, the twenty-five stripes she cut into my shoulders.

"So pretty," she says.

She takes the clips off one at a time. We've been together over five weeks now. I see her four or five days a week, sometimes more, sometimes less. We don't always do this. We go to movies. We go dancing. We shop for fabric and groceries and I keep her company while she sews. I go to her house and I make her breakfast and sit on the floor next to her chair, working on my articles, while she manages her affairs, her husband at work in the city. We do other things, but this is what we're doing now.

I try to breathe deeply as she removes the clips. The clips on my penis hurt so much. I've made it much worse with small movements. It's hard for me to stay still. "Oh, god," I say when she pulls the clips from my penis in one motion, tugging the rope, like a zipper. Everything is white for a second. There's this sound I'm making and I'm in the back of my head watching myself. "Come back to me," I hear. It's a voice so far away.

When my vision returns, Eden is there. "Hi," she says. She's smiling. "You took a lot." I want to tell her that I once rode a bus late at night when I was thirteen. Everything was purple and yellow. The acid was so strong at four in the morning I thought the police officer was Napoleon. My friend's father picked us up when the sun came out and he took my friend home and I walked down Devon Avenue into Little India and scaled a drainpipe onto a roof and slept the morning covered in cardboard boxes. I want to tell her that when I was in fifth grade I was so good at dodgeball I was the best in my class. I played soccer, chess. I want to brag, stand on my hands. I want to impress her.

But she keeps her eyes on me and I don't say anything. She pulls a bar from her pocket, slides a square of chocolate between my lips and I start to cry.

I'm still lying on the hard floor when Eden suggests untying me. "No," I say. "Please." I'm worried that my crying will make her stop. When I've been with women and cried before, they always stopped. I don't want her to stop. I don't want her to go. So she holds me for a while and then slides out from under me, rolling me onto my side, pressing her hand across my face.

She hits me first on my left cheek. She's still smiling but my vision is going again. I'm crawling into my head, tucking into that little room. I have no right to be here. I have never done anything to deserve someone like Eden. The slaps get harder, and then the other side. I'm not in the same place anymore. I try to see Eden but she disappears and it's just the hard slaps on my cheek, and soon she is replaced with an image of my father. He's wearing his green bomber jacket. There's snow all around us. He's holding me by the neck, walking me back into the house. The social worker called from school. I've been sick from sleeping outside. The cold has seeped into my bones and I sit in my eighth-grade class shivering through the day. I'm always cold. The first slap comes over by the fireplace. My sister is upstairs sleeping. My mother is dead four months now. We're right by the couch she spent the last years of her life on, virtually paralyzed and left alone most of the day with her small black-and-white TV. I miss her so much and I don't even know it yet. I haven't even begun to really think about her. She died and I left but now the social workers have called and my father is angry so he tracked me down. I've been telling lies about the family. I've betrayed him. I've made him look bad, done him wrong. This is what is coming to me. This is what I have brought on myself.

Eden is hitting me so hard, cradling the other side of my head in her hand. The animal I sound like doesn't exist yet. Like a strange beast dying in the forest. My father's pulling me to the kitchen. There's clippers there. He's shaving my head. I'm paralyzed with fear. Her ropes are biting into me and I can't move. I just see him now. Just my father, with no background, his green bomber jacket. Why didn't I fight back? Because I've always been a coward.

And then he's replaced with another image, a year later. The state has taken custody. I was found with my wrists cut open, sleeping in an entryway. They asked me where my parents were; I told them I didn't know. They moved. I'm in a group home, just turned fifteen. There's a house meeting in the living room. I'm standing, holding a butter knife. The biggest boy in the home hits me open-handed across the face. "What are you going to do now?" he says. We're all wards of the court. We have nothing to lose. We shuttle from homes to institutions, between mental hospitals and jails. The staff stays seated, watching to see how this plays out. I could use some help.

I'm crying so hard and I can't stop. These are not the tears of love.

"Look at me." My eyes have been closed. Her face is there. Still kind. I don't even know what's happening. "Keep your eyes open." Her hand is still on my cheek. I can't seem to keep my eyes open. When I do, I keep crying. I want to scream and keep screaming. I want to say *No!* I try to close my eyes, to find my own head.

"Look at me."

What happened? I ask myself, but I know perfectly well what happened to me. I keep waiting for it to not have happened. Eden keeps saying she wants to give a space to that little boy inside me. Last time I spoke with my father, he said that was eighteen years ago already. It's time you get over it. I don't get over anything. I'm staring at Eden and I'm cracked into a million pieces. I want to do something for her. I don't even know what I could do.

I cry for so long. She has a gas mask in her bag. "I want to put this on you," she says. I push my face up toward it. I have rope burn between my legs. "I'm not going to put this on you yet, but I will soon." So I cry for a while longer but eventually I stop, and then the mask comes on. I can't tell when she's holding the mask closed except when I exhale and can't breathe back in. She keeps doing this until I'm panicking. We've been going for hours now. She holds her breath with me. She knows I should be able to hold my breath longer.

We don't know that her husband has been leaving messages on my phone. Her mother is OK. Her mother doesn't have cancer. It's just scar tissue. The phone is turned off. I can't breathe and I'm shaking my head, no no no no. And she's saying, "Are you saying no to me?" and I'm saying no, I'm not saying no to you, so I lie still and take what she wants to give me, which is what I always do when I think she's going too far—stretch myself out, take more, just to hear her say, "Good boy." It's the only thing in the world worth hearing.

And when she's done she finally unties me, and I am stiff and sore and we lie in bed together. "It makes me wet to hit you," she says, and I slide my hand inside her pants to feel where her panties are damp. I rub her there. "I was so far gone," I say. "I was totally gone."

"You were, you were gone."

"Nobody's ever been as nice to me as you," I say.

"You haven't been hanging out with the right people."

Since meeting her I've wondered what it would have been like if I had met her earlier. Would I have been ready to accept what she offers? Would I still have been raped in a hotel room; done coke off a table while a man dressed in a nurse's outfit went down on three homeless men near Lake Michigan? Would I have accomplished anything; would I have needed to?

Eventually we go to dinner, but first we check my phone and find that her husband has called, and her mom, and David—the boy she owns, who goes with her to the clubs and carries her things. They've all called. How strange, I think, to be part of this family. They're all calling with the good news.

"I could cry," Eden says, but she doesn't.

At the restaurant we hold hands. This is one of our resolutions, to go out more. I suggest calling some friends, but neither of us wants to. Instead we go back to my apartment.

"I'm just setting you up," Eden says. "I'm going to leave you." She's teasing.

"You're stepping on my emotional wires," I tell her.

We're not done. She lays a towel on my bed. "On your back," she says. I wonder if we need to do this. How are we connecting? Through our bodies, psychological closets we weren't supposed to open. But I don't care because I'll go wherever she wants to go.

I've given her the top drawer of my dresser and she keeps an extra shirt in there, a box of latex gloves, my collar, a large bottle of lube, rubbers, dental dams, a bracelet I made her from amber. I don't cry when she pushes her finger into my ass. I've written love stories before but they've never been happy. I wrote a whole book about the urge to substitute abuse for affection. The last girl I dated had me call her Daddy, hit me from anger when we were walking down the street, kicked me out of her apartment in the middle of the night—and I walked home from there and witnessed a car crash while standing beneath the overhang of a convenience store wondering what I should do.

"When you write," Eden says, "you make yourself sound damaged and you insist that you're a coward. But you're not. You're strong." Maybe if she keeps telling me that I'll believe it, but I'm not ready for that yet.

Even with all the lube, it hurts, her hand in my ass. And then I fall asleep. I go. I have nothing left. I dream for moments and then forget my dreams awakening to the sharp pain of her withdrawal. "Talk to me for a while," she says. "How did it feel?"

"It felt good," I say. But I'm always afraid when she does that.

"I felt you go to sleep," she says. "I felt your body loosen up."

I try to talk to her more but I can't. In the morning my flight is so early and I'll be gone for so long. Twelve days. It seems forever but I'm almost feeling like I can make it—though I know it'll only take me a day to change my mind about that. But there are no options. Even if I stayed she'd have to spend the next two days with her son and husband and then on Sunday she leaves for a week. I could stay but I can't make her stay.

"Touch me," she says. It's six in the morning. The sun is lighting my curtains. I slide my fingers between her legs. "I smell like garlic down there. From the meat loaf last night."

"You have garlic cooch," I say. She hasn't shaved her legs, her armpits. I think of Frank Zappa singing *Give me your dirty love*. This is not something I would have done—joked about body fluids, made love in the morning before brushing my teeth, but this is what I do now. I don't care anything about who I was before. That person is gone.

She drives me to the airport. The highways are clear across the bay and I stroke her leg crossing over the bridge. We're early so we sit in the short-term parking lot. "Imagine a lake in front of us," I say. "We're on a cliff, surrounded by trees. The sky is like velvet, covered in stars." She reaches across my waist, slides my seat back, climbs into my lap.

When it's time she walks me to the gate. "This is so romantic," I say. "You took me to the airport. You're walking me to the terminal. It's like going steady."

"Does that mean I get a ring?" she asks. She has rings. She has a wedding ring, an engagement ring. Last night in the restaurant we were talking about the war and I told her I was a British citizen and that when it came to it we'd move somewhere in the Commonwealth, keep her safe. I wasn't talking about her husband but she thought I was.

"We'd have to get married for that to be true," she said.

I wanted to tell her I was only joking, but I didn't. I said, "I could marry you." And what I meant was that maybe, if we were together five years from now, we could have a ceremony, or something. It didn't matter.

"I don't believe in divorce," she said, sticking her fork into her food. The owner of the restaurant is an old friend of mine but he wasn't there. I was drinking a beer. "For me I don't believe in it, I mean."

Inside the terminal we're running out of time. We kiss, and then we kiss some more.

"You made me cry feeding me chocolate," I say.

"You were so pretty."

There is nothing left except platitudes, all of them true. *I love you. I'll miss you. I'll think about you every day. I'll call. I'll email. I'll see you again.*

I feel clear stepping through the checkpoint. The plane is already boarding. The truth is that everything is fine. Even Eden's husband has grown comfortable with the situation. He's agreed that Eden can sleep over at my house once a week starting when I get back. The future is bright. This is a happy story.

Epilogue:
My Mainstream Girlfriend

LISTEN. I ALWAYS THOUGHT I WAS KINKY. I've always read bondage porn and jerked off to videos of women wrestling or stories of teachers blackmailed into sexual servitude by their students. I used to stand in the bookstore rereading Eric Stanton comics until I finally saved the eighty dollars to buy the Taschen coffee-table book. But yesterday my girlfriend came over and something happened that made me think I might not be kinky anymore. She was wearing ruby slippers, like Dorothy in *The Wizard of Oz.* But she was also wearing torn fishnets with a garter belt, sexy underwear, a long black dress over a lacy slip. A lot of women would feel self-conscious dressed so sexy, but I have an awesome girlfriend.

We do a lot of stuff that some people might think is outside the mainstream. Like, we'll go to a party and she'll sit on the couch and point to the floor and I'll sit on the floor in front of her. It's a power thing. There'll be colleagues from the university I teach at, other writers. Some of my friends think it's weird. But it's not really that weird. Also, sometimes she'll put a collar on my neck and I'll wear it around the house. I talked to my roommates about it. I told them to keep in mind that I clean the bathroom when she comes over, so if they want a clean bathroom they have to be OK with the other stuff.

Often she'll spank me really hard, or hit me with a whip. If she wants me to be emotionally vulnerable she'll kick me out of the bed and make me sleep on the floor for a while. It doesn't take long before I start to break. I'm not an emotionally strong person. A lot of times when she ties me up and she's hurting me, smacking my balls or my face or pulling really hard on my nipples, I'll start to cry. I'll think about my father or some of the things that happened when I was a kid. It's called trauma play: I eroticize my childhood abuse.

One time I cried when she had her hand in my ass. We had only just started dating. I was lying on a towel on my back and she was looking at me, watching me closely. She was wearing a latex glove and using a lot of lube. She slid one finger in, then another. I felt her reach inside me, curl her fingers. I started to panic. I told her it hurt. It burned. It always hurt but it was just two fingers. How much could a finger hurt? I told her I was worried. I confessed I was worried that I was dirty, that there would be shit on her finger. I didn't even know it until I said it but the truth rolled across me like a plow. Then I told her I was more worried about that than anything in the world and I started crying and I cried for a long time. I thought, Man, I am so fucked up.

"I'm sorry," was all I could say. "Please don't leave."

She kept her hand inside me, stroking my hair with her other hand. "Look at me," she said. She was leaning in close to me and I could see that she loved me on every line in her face. "I think you're amazing," she said, and I cried some more.

But now I don't feel so self-conscious about my ass. Freud take note, maybe my girlfriend has taken me out of the anal stage? Recently she's been fucking me with a strap-on. Which is what she did yesterday.

I've been fucked with a strap-on before. Often a really small one or just very briefly. Normally I start screaming right away: "It hurts! It hurts! It hurts!" That hasn't always stopped the other person.

The first time I really open up to her she has me tied to the table in the middle of my room. She's good with knots, and she has lots of rope. Admittedly, being tied to a table and ass-fucked is pretty kinky. And it was only a week ago. And my whole point here is that maybe I'm not that kinky anymore, but I'm getting to that. I'm not there yet. Stay with me. So she's fucking me. She goes in really slow, whispering me through it. "There's no hurry," she says. And for the first time it really doesn't hurt. I can feel her going in and out of me and it just feels good. The cock is probably seven or eight inches long and average width. I can feel my asshole stretched around it. She's picking up speed. I get this whole euphoric feeling. Like I'm on ecstasy or something. It washes across me. I feel so good. I feel great. I'm in love with everybody, and with my girlfriend in particular. My arms are pulled forward, nipple clamps run from my nipples to my wrists. The clamps pull on my nipples every time she slams into my ass. And I start talking all dirty. I'm like, "Oh, yeah. Please. Fuck. Me. Fuck me. Fuck me." Like I'm in a porno or something. But it feels good to say. And she likes it.

I couldn't believe it didn't hurt.

So what happened yesterday is that my girlfriend came over dressed all sexy. There's nothing kinky, I think, about admiring a woman who is dressed sexy. And she's great looking all the time anyway. I mean, my girl-friend is super-hot. I'm not saying she's not really smart, interesting, political, compelling, or caring. She is. But that's not what I'm talking about here. What I'm trying to say is that my girlfriend has the kind of body that could stop a train. I'm lucky. She likes me. What am I supposed to do about that? Talk her out of it? No way.

So she came over and she wanted to fuck me. She's leaving for two weeks to rebuild a Buddhist temple in Mississippi and she wanted to have sex before she left and by sex she meant she wanted to fuck my ass. I hadn't known she was coming over and there was still a small piece of rope on the floor from the last time she tied me to the table and the table was still in the center of the room. I apologized for that and she hit me a couple of times with the rope. Then I went down on her.

Then she spread a towel on my bed and lubed up my ass. We use Liquid Silk. Elbo Grease lasts longer but Liquid Silk seems to work better. At least that's been our experience together. Maybe different lubes work differently on different assholes. Hard to say.

She takes off her dress and her slip rises and falls across her knees. She takes that off and it's just her beautiful vintage underwear, the naked tops of her thighs and her torn fishnets with the ivory garter and ruby slippers. I watch her put the harness on, sliding the black silicone cock into its binding, pulling the rubber over the head. "OK," she says. "Ass up in the air."

She's fucking me again. She told me before that every guy wants something in his ass. She's a sex worker so she would know. Apparently it's the big secret among men, the thing men don't talk about with each other. I brought it up earlier in the week with my friend Josh. Josh is a science writer and I was staying at his house in Los Angeles for a couple of days. There was a party I was down there for. I shook Bill Maher's hand. That's another story. But the point is I mentioned this to Josh, that my girlfriend had told me every guy wants something in his ass. He explained that there were all these nerve endings and that the prostate was like a male G-spot. He was dropping me off at the Burbank airport and I got the impression, though he didn't come right out and say it, that he enjoyed having things in his ass, too. So I figure my girlfriend is right. She usually is. So you see what I'm saying? Nothing so kinky about what we're doing here. She's fucking me in the ass and it feels really good but then every guy wants something in his ass.

I look back at her. She's still wearing her ruby slippers with their little heels. She has one knee down and the other knee up, like she's being knighted. Her left foot is planted firmly on the bed to give her leverage and she's gripping me by the hips, pulling me back into her. All I can see are her shoes and her legs in her fishnets. I wish I had a picture of it. On my end I'm just trying to keep the rhythm. I can't help but let out all these little moans of pleasure. I'm having a really good time. Here's what makes me think I'm not kinky anymore. This time, instead of thinking about my father and all the bad stuff that happened when I was younger, I'm thinking about what she looks like fucking me. I'm also thinking about a hamburger and a chocolate shake. I'm being fucked and it feels really good and I'm thinking, Oh man, I would *love* a chocolate shake right now. It's a deep hunger, a deep sex hunger. That's not just normal, that's all-American.

After she fucks me for a while and I get that my-girl-friend-fucked-the-hell-out-of-me glow, I go down on her some more. She slips her underwear off and puts her dress back on and then hikes it up, lowering her ass onto my face. I'm surrounded by her magnificent ass. With her dress over me her pussy and ass are my entire world. I'm eating her out, her legs pinning my arms. I'm ravenous for her. I love the way she tastes. I didn't used to like the way a woman tastes but my girlfriend cured me of that. I want to get my tongue deep inside of her. I want to lick her heart. I go down on her for so long that the next day my neck hurts.

So there it is. I thought I was so kinky, so alternative. But really I'm just a guy who appreciates sexy clothes, likes something in his ass, and loves going down on his girlfriend. After sex I like a big meal. Normal.

There was one thing. Since she was leaving for a while she carved POSSESSION in my side with the knife she keeps by my bed. She says she needs to sharpen it. She's been using it too much and it's getting dull. But she wanted me to be able to look in the mirror and think of her while she's gone. Also, in case I met another woman, that other woman would know there was already someone in my life when she saw POSSESSION recently cut into my skin. It's like those stickers on aspirin bottles that let you know this product was packaged for Walgreens and if you're buying it anywhere else you're taking part in some sort of crime. Labeling. I admit it, a lot of people aren't comfortable with cutting. Cutting is still "kinky." I have all these marks all over me from where she's cut me. But really, it's a small thing. I spend much more time with my face between her legs than I do getting cut. You have to look at the percentages. More and more I feel like I'm joining mainstream America.

About the Author

STEPHEN ELLIOTT is the author of five books includ-
ing *Happy Baby*, a finalist for the New York Public
Library's Young Lion Award as well as a best book of
2004 in Salon.com, *Newsday, Chicago New City*, the
Journal News, and the *Village Voice*. His work has been
featured in *Esquire*, the *New York Times, GQ, Best
American Non-Required Reading, Best American
Erotica*, and *Best Sex Writing*. He is the founder of the
Progressive Reading Series and the executive director
of LitPAC, a literary political action committee. He lives
in San Francisco and can be found on the Web at
www.stephenelliott.com.